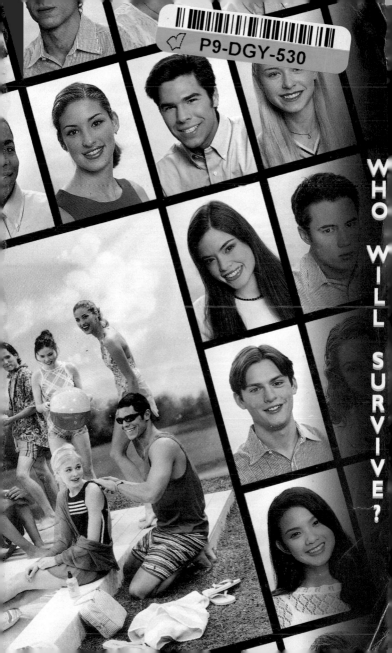

P9-DGY-530

WHO WILL SURVIVE?

IT'S GOING
TO BE A
KILLER
YEAR!

Is the senior class at Shadyside High doomed? That's the prediction Trisha Conrad makes at her summer party—and it looks as if she may be right. Spend a year with the FEAR STREET seniors, as each month in this new 12-book series brings horror after horror. Will anyone reach graduation day alive?

Only R.L. Stine knows...

Mira Block

LIKES:
Going to clubs, guys in bands, sexy clothes

REMEMBERS:
The cemetery, senior camp-out, hanging out with Clarissa

HATES:
Waifs, talking on the phone, psychics

QUOTE:
"Don't hate me 'cause I'm beautiful."

Greta Bradley

LIKES:
Cheerleading, football games, all my close friends

REMEMBERS:
The social, he asked me out, shopping at Chanel with Jade

HATES:
Ceramics, empty times, New Year's Eve

QUOTE:
"That boy is mine."

REST IN PEACE

Trisha Conrad

LIKES:
Shopping in the mall my dad owns, giving fabulous parties, Gary Fresno

REMEMBERS:
The murder game, the senior table at Pete's Pizza

HATES:
Rich girl jokes, bad karma, overalls

QUOTE:
"What you don't know will hurt you."

Danielle Cortez

LIKES:
My cat, little kids, cheering the Tigers, dancing

REMEMBERS:
Trisha's party, finally making varsity cheerleader

HATES:
The first day of school, being cold, rivals

QUOTE:
"Push 'em down, push 'em down, push 'em waaaay down! Go Tigers!"

REST IN PEACE

Clark Dickson

LIKES:
Debra Lake, poetry, painting

REMEMBERS:
Trisha's party, the first time I saw Debra

HATES:
Nicknames, dentists, garlic pizza, tans

QUOTE:
"Fangs for the memories."

Jennifer Fear

LIKES:
Basketball, antique jewelry, cool music

REMEMBERS:
The doom spell, senior cut day, hanging with Trisha and Josie

HATES:
The way people are afraid of the Fears, pierced eyebrows

QUOTE:
"There's nothing to fear but fear itself."

Jade Feldman

LIKES:
Cheerleading, expensive clothes, working

REMEMBERS:
Ice skating, senior cut day, dances with Dana

HATES:
Cheerleading tryouts, gym, contact lenses

QUOTE:
"You get what you pay for."

REST IN PEACE

Gary Fresno

LIKES:
Hanging out by the bleachers, art class, gym

REMEMBERS:
Cruisin' down Division Street with the guys, that special night with that special person (you know who you are...)

HATES:
My beat-up Civic, working after school everyday, cops

QUOTE:
"Don't judge a book by its cover."

Kenny Klein

LIKES:
Jade Feldman, chemistry, Latin, baseball

REMEMBERS:
The first time I beat Marla Newman in a debate, Junior Prom with Jade

HATES:
Nine-year-olds who like to torture camp counselors, cafeteria food

QUOTE:
"Look before you leap."

Debra Lake

LIKES:
Sensitive ~~~~, Clark's poems

REMEMBERS:
Basketball games, when Clark painted my portrait

HATES:
Possessive boyfriends and jealous girlfriends

QUOTE:
"I would do anything for you, but I won't do that."

Stacy Malcolm

LIKES:
Sports, funky hats, shopping

REMEMBERS:
Running laps with Mary, stuffing our faces at Pete's, Mr. Morley and Rob

HATES:
Psycho killers, stealing boyfriends

QUOTE:
"College, here I come!"

Josh Maxwell

LIKES:
Debra Lake, Debra Lake, Debra Lake

REMEMBERS:
Hanging out at the old mill, senior camp-out, Coach's pep talks

HATES:
Funeral homes, driving my parents' car, tomato juice

QUOTE:
"Sometimes you don't realize the truth until it bites you right on the neck."

Josie Maxwell

LIKES:
Black clothes, black nail polish, black lipstick, photography

REMEMBERS:
Trisha's first senior party, the memorial wall

HATES:
Algebra, evil spirits (including Marla Newman), being compared to my stepbrother Josh

QUOTE:
"The past isn't always the past—sometimes it's the future."

Mickey Myers

LIKES:
Jammin' with the band, partying, hot girls

REMEMBERS:
Swimming in Fear Lake, the storm, my first gig at the Underground

HATES:
Dweebs, studying, girls who diet, station wagons

QUOTE:
"Shadyside High rules!"

Marla Newman

LIKES:
Writing, cool clothes, being a redhead

REMEMBERS:
Yearbook deadlines, competing with Kenny Klein, when Josie put a spell on me (ha ha)

HATES:
Girls who wear all black, guys with long hair, the dark arts

QUOTE:
"The power is divided when the circle is not round."

Mary O'Connor

LIKES:
Running, ripped jeans, hair spray

REMEMBERS:
Not being invited to Trisha's party, rat poison

HATES:
Social studies, rich girls, cliques

QUOTE:
"Just say no."

Dana Palmer

LIKES:
Boys, boys, boys, cheerleading, short skirts

REMEMBERS:
Senior camp-out with Mickey, Homecoming, the back seat

HATES:
Private cheerleading performances, fire batons, sharing clothes

QUOTE:
"The bad twin always wins!"

Deirdre Palmer

LIKES:
Mysterious guys, sharing clothes, old movies

REMEMBERS:
The cabin in the Fear Street woods, sleepovers at Jen's

HATES:
Being a "good girl," sweat socks

QUOTE:
"What you see isn't always what you get."

Will Reynolds

LIKES:
The Turner family, playing guitar, clubbing

REMEMBERS:
The first time Clarissa saw me without my dreads, our booth at Pete's

HATES:
Lite FM, the clinic, lilacs

QUOTE:
"I get knocked down, but I get up again…"

Ty Sullivan

LIKES:
Ch ses ears, m ous, brains, football

RE
he graveyard with you w o, Ke dein's lucky shot

HATES:
Painting ces, entine's Day

QUOTE:
"The more the merrier."

Justin Thompson

LIKES:
Computers, the Beastie Boys, Barry White

REMEMBERS:
Don't want to remember anything about Shadyside

HATES:
Having my face shoved in the toilet, being chased by Ty and Gary

QUOTE:
"You're my everything."

Clarissa Turner

LIKES:
Art, music, talking on the phone

REMEMBERS:
Shopping with Debra, my first day back to school, eating pizza with Will

HATES:
Mira Block

QUOTE:
"Real friendship never dies."

Matty Winger

LIKES:
Computers, video games, Star Trek

REMEMBERS:
The murder game—good one Trisha

HATES:
People who can't take a joke, finding Clark's cape with Josh

QUOTE:
"Don't worry, be happy."

Phoebe Yamura

LIKES:
Cheerleading, gymnastics, big crowds

REMEMBERS:
That awesome game against Waynesbridge, senior trip, tailgate parties

HATES:
When people don't give it their all, liars, vans

QUOTE:
"Today is the first day of the rest of our lives."

R.L. Stine
Seniors
A Fear Street Super Chiller

episode nine Spring
Break

A Parachute Press Book

A GOLD KEY PAPERBACK
Golden Books Publishing Company, Inc.
New York

Check out the new FEAR STREET® Website
http://www.fearstreet.com

A Gold Key Paperback Original

Golden Books Publishing Company, Inc.
888 Seventh Avenue
New York, NY 10106

ISBN: 0-307-24713-9

First Gold Key paperback printing March 1999

10   9   8   7   6   5   4   3   2   1

Photographer: Jimmy Levin

Printed in the U.S.A.

PART ONE

ow. Check out the red and yellow sand. That's a real desert down there," Josh Maxwell said excitedly.

Mickey Myers leaned over Josh to peer out of the plane window. "See any camels?"

Josh laughed. "I don't think they have camels in Arizona."

Mickey looked disappointed.

The big 737 jet had begun its descent. They were minutes away from Tucson International Airport. Josh knew that Trisha Conrad was waiting there to pick them up and drive them to her family's ranch.

"Thanks for the great scenery, Trisha!" Mickey exclaimed. "Trisha thinks of everything."

"Hey—Trisha is great!" Josh added. "Who

1

else could put all of us up for spring break?"

Mickey brushed back his sandy hair and grinned. "Or who else could put *up* with us?"

Across the aisle Deirdre Palmer giggled. "Trisha is *glad* we're coming. She said the ranch gets boring when she's there alone."

"Works for me," Josh said, stretching. He'd been friends with Trisha Conrad since the fifth grade—good friends. Her family had tons of money, but Trisha never acted superior toward anyone. Instead, she was sweet. Generous.

"Too bad about Dana," Mickey muttered.

Dana Palmer, Deirdre's twin sister, had caught the flu the day before spring break began. Her parents made her stay home. Which had put Mickey in a bad mood. He wasn't thrilled about spending spring break without her.

"Dana was bummed," Deirdre said, shaking her head. "But there's no way she could get on a plane with a fever."

"Bad timing," Mickey murmured unhappily.

"Yeah." Josh leaned forward to pull his sunglasses out of his backpack. "Spring break . . ."

". . . has officially begun," Gary Fresno chimed in. He strolled up the aisle holding a tray of snack bags. "Who wants peanuts? Pretzels?"

Mickey waved his arms. "Hey—pretzels. Heave it!"

Gary dropped the tray onto an empty seat. Like a pitcher on the mound, Gary whipped one arm back.

"There's the windup—" Josh said, mimicking a sports announcer. "And the fast ball!"

The pretzel bag shot through the air. Mickey snagged it in one hand.

"Excuse me!"

A flight attendant hurried up the aisle. "I need that," she snapped, grabbing the tray. "And you need to sit down. We're landing."

Gary waved the attendant off. "Yeah. Whatever."

"Please, sir," the woman insisted. "The captain has turned on the seat belt sign."

But Gary didn't move. *"Sir?"* he repeated, making a face.

The attendant bit her lower lip. Definitely annoyed, but trying not to show it.

"Come on, Gary," Josh said. "We'll be on the ground in ten minutes."

Gary shrugged. "That's Gary, sir!" he declared. Then he squeezed past Deirdre to his seat.

Josh pressed his head against the padded seat. He wasn't in the mood for trouble. A good time—yes. A wild time—maybe. But there'd be plenty of opportunity to let loose once they settled in at the ranch.

Horseback riding. Swimming. Tennis. Some hikes through the desert.

Far away from Shadyside. From the high school where so many strange accidents and horrible deaths had been stalking his class. It felt so nice to be far away from all that. . . .

"I see hills," Mickey said, leaning over Josh to see out the window, deliberately digging his fist into Josh's leg. "And sand. And those weird green trees with thorns all over."

Josh shoved Mickey away. "Try cactuses."

"Get ready for some fireworks," Gary Fresno called across the aisle. "There's bound to be a few explosions when Trisha's parents find out that *I'm* one of the guests."

"Don't even say that!" Deirdre exclaimed.

It was no secret that Trisha's parents disliked Gary Fresno. Mr. and Mrs. Conrad didn't want their daughter hanging around with a guy who lived on the "other side" of Division Street.

A guy with an earring and an attitude.

But despite her parents' angry protests, Trisha was drawn to Gary. She seemed to be crazy about him.

That didn't surprise Josh. Gary was a wild man. A fun guy to have around.

"The Conrads are in Australia," Josh pointed out.

"Yeah," Mickey added. "Even if they find out about Gary, it's sort of hard to ground Trisha from the other side of the world."

"Which leaves us free. To par-tee!" Gary crowed.

Josh stared out the window. The plane lowered over hills and roads and scorched sand. He felt the wheels bump hard on the runway. Then the plane began to roll smoothly.

"Welcome to Tucson International," the flight attendant announced.

Outside, waves of heat shimmered over the landing strip.

Josh slipped on his sunglasses. "Let's do it!"

Ignoring the instructions of the flight attendant, Gary unbuckled his seat belt and pressed into the aisle as the plane reached the terminal.

"Got to find Trisha," Gary called back before he disappeared in a line of bobbing heads and luggage.

"Is he in a hurry, or what?" Deirdre asked.

"Gary waits for no one," Josh said as he pulled his backpack out from under the seat.

Together Josh, Mickey, and Deirdre filed out of the plane and wove through the crowded terminal. Through a long corridor. Down an escalator. Through another corridor.

To the baggage claim area. The luggage wasn't coming out yet.

Good thing, Josh thought. Since Gary and Trisha were both sitting on the edge of the conveyor belt, arms around each other.

"When that thing starts up, you two are going to end up in the parking lot!" Josh exclaimed.

Trisha sprang up, pulling Gary alongside her.

"Hey, guys! You made it!" Smiling, Trisha used her sunglasses to push back her streaked blond hair. She wore denim shorts and a white tank top that showed off her tan.

"Hey!" Deirdre gave her a gentle shove. "You've been logging in some serious pooltime."

"It's been rough." Trisha sighed. "Good thing you guys are here. Someone has to save me

5

before I get deep-fried."

A loud buzzer made everyone step back. The conveyor belt began to roll. Suitcases and boxes plunged through the hanging flaps and lurched by the waiting passengers.

"There's my stuff!" Deirdre pointed to two pieces of luggage covered with a tapestry design. She turned to Mickey. "Do you mind? They're kind of heavy."

"No problem." Mickey turned his maroon Shadyside baseball cap around and followed her up to the conveyor belt.

Josh's black duffel bag shot onto the belt. He circled two kids wheeling a luggage cart and brushed past an elderly couple near an empty spot on the belt.

He was reaching down when someone bumped his shoulder.

Josh spun around and found himself breathing into the face of a rough-looking guy. Big. Powerful-looking. Probably in his twenties. He wore jeans and a black Stetson hat.

"Excuse me," Josh muttered. He turned back toward his bag, but something blocked his path. He tripped.

And his sneaker tromped on top of the big guy's foot.

The guy growled. "Hey! Would you give me a break—!"

"Sorry!" Josh stepped away. His bag was rushing by.

He reached toward the belt. . . .

Just as the big guy leaned down.

Josh's arm shot out, knocking the guy's Stetson hat to the floor.

"Sorry," Josh called, catching his bag.

A woman pushed in beside him. She heaved her bag off the conveyor belt. And dropped it onto the Stetson.

Josh stared down at the crushed hat. The woman lugged her suitcase away, not even seeing the hat.

The big guy wheeled around furiously. Without his hat his face was square and solid. He had a flattop haircut and a moon-shaped scar on his forehead.

An angry scar.

"I'm sorry, man," Josh said.

"You keep saying that." The guy pointed at Josh. As if accusing him.

"Hey!" Josh stepped back. "What's your problem?"

"You're my problem now."

Josh held up his hands. "It was an accident. I mean, I'm sorry about your hat, but—"

"You've got a sorry excuse for everything," the big guy growled. "Don't you?" He thrust a beefy fist onto Josh's chest. "Don't you? *Don't you!"*

"Look—" Josh gasped as the guy shoved him again. Why was this moron making such a big deal out of nothing? "Can't we talk about—"

"I'm through with talking." His big hand grasped the front of Josh's shirt. He got a grip—and pulled.

Josh's sneakers dragged against the floor.

7

The smell of sweat and beer were strong. This guy was out of control. Drunk and out of control.

"Just back off, *okay?*" Josh demanded shrilly. His heart started to pound.

How crazy *is* this guy?

"I'll back off," the stranger growled, hauling Josh away. "Just as soon as we settle this outside."

Chapter TWO

One Angry Cowboy

N o way! Josh thought.
No way!
A fistfight. With a psycho. A psycho who's been drinking.

Josh could think of a million better ways to start his vacation.

Desperately he twisted around. They were getting closer to the exit. And if the psycho made it outside, away from security . . . anything could happen.

I've got to get away *now,* Josh decided.

The guy was strong, but Josh surprised him by ducking suddenly. He slipped loose and scrambled away.

"Get back here, wimp!" the guy roared.

"Josh! Hey—Josh!"

Josh spun around to see Deirdre chasing after him. "Josh . . . what's going on?"

9

Mickey rushed up behind her, his eyes flashing from Josh to the beefy stranger. Summing up the situation, he said, "Time to go."

Deirdre linked her arm through Josh's and pulled him away. "Are you okay?"

"Yeah, let's get out of here," Josh said. Quickly he helped Mickey grab the bags.

The cowboy glared at Josh. Ready to pounce.

"You wanna mess with Clay Hartley?" he called, slurring the words, his face bright red. "Okay, cowboy. I'm watching you."

"Don't encourage him," Deirdre warned Josh as they hustled to the exit. "Don't say anything. And don't look back."

"Trisha went to get the car," Mickey said. "She's meeting us by that door."

"Where's Gary?" Josh asked.

"He found a candy machine outside," Deirdre reported. "He's loading up on Snickers bars."

The glass door slid open, and Josh plunged into dry, hot air. After a drab winter in Shadyside, the sunshine felt great.

"Where are you going?" Gary asked. He stood by a vending machine, a half-eaten candy bar in his hand. Two others were jammed in his shirt pocket. "I saw that guy steamroll you! Let's give him a little attitude adjustment."

Josh swung back toward the doors of the terminal. "No way!" he cried. "That guy is *big*. I just want to get away from here."

"Trisha is waiting." Deirdre pointed to the

10

end of the crosswalk.

Trisha waved from the driver's seat of a huge Mercedes van. Quickly the kids stowed their gear in the back and climbed in.

Trisha adjusted her sunglasses and turned to Josh. "You okay?"

He nodded.

"Ten minutes in Arizona and you're already in a showdown," she teased. "I can't take you guys anywhere."

"Just get us out of here," Josh said as everyone buckled up.

"You got it." Trisha eased the van into gear.

Josh let out a sigh and started to relax as they rolled into the bright sunlight.

"Nice wheels . . ." Mickey whistled.

"Yeah." Josh ran his hand over a smooth leather armrest. That was Trisha. She traveled in style.

As they drove, Trisha pointed out some of the sights. Josh thought it all looked a lot like home. Office buildings, golf courses, and shopping centers . . .

"Hey—" Josh called to Trisha. "Where'd you put the desert?"

She laughed. "Tucson is a city. There's a university here. And a film studio. And tons of tourists. But you'll get your share of red rock and sand. Our ranch is outside town. Smack in the middle of the Sonoran Desert."

Josh leaned back. This was the way to spend spring break. Soaking up sunshine. Cruising with friends.

Turning in his seat, he gazed out at cactus clusters and small adobe houses. Traffic was light on the four-lane highway. But a black convertible was speeding up behind them, closing in.

"Watch it," he called out to Trisha. "Some hotshot is running his own race."

He turned back as the black car shot closer. . . .

Roaring . . . tearing up the roadway . . .

"This guy's got to be doing a hundred!" he said.

He stared out the back, watching the car roar closer.

"Whoa—!"

The driver.

It couldn't be! The square, red face. The flat-top hair. The furious eyes.

Josh's throat suddenly felt tight and dry.

"The creep from the airport!" Josh cried. "What's he doing?"

"He's driving like a maniac!" Deirdre shouted.

"He *is* a maniac!" Mickey exclaimed.

The black car roared closer. Closer . . .

"He's going to hit us!" Josh cried. "Look out—!"

The black convertible smashed into them. Hard.

Josh felt himself being thrown forward. The seat belt caught him and pulled him back.

The impact sent the van skidding onto the shoulder. Trisha frantically yanked the wheel to the left.

Josh struggled to catch his breath.

Dust swirled all around them.

The van bumped through the dust . . . then swerved back onto the road.

"He hit us! I don't believe it! That jerk deliberately hit us!" Gary shouted. He turned to Trisha and asked, "Hey—you okay?"

She nodded, keeping her eyes on the road.

"Get his license number!" Deirdre steadied herself, then reached into her backpack for something to write with. "Can you see his license tag?"

Josh stared through the shimmering heat and dust. "There's no plate on the front of the car."

Trisha gripped the wheel hard, leaning over it tensely. She checked her mirror and cried, "He's coming back!"

"This guy is totally messed up!" Josh screamed, bracing himself. "Look out! He's—"

WHAM!

The black car bumped their van again.

"What's his problem?" Mickey asked.

Josh shook his head. "I don't get it. What did I do to him? I mean, why won't he leave us alone?"

WHAM!

Josh lurched forward, then back, as the convertible slammed into them again.

The crazy driver pointed furiously at Josh. He waved frantically, signaling for Trisha to pull over.

"He wants us to stop!" Deirdre cried.

"For what?" Josh couldn't believe this guy. "So he can beat up all of us?"

Gary raised a fist in the air. "Hey! We've got him outnumbered! We can take this dude!"

"No way," Trisha said firmly.

Deirdre shook her head. Panic filled her eyes. "Keep going, Trisha. We can't stop! Someone will get hurt. Something awful will happen."

The drunken cowboy honked his horn again and again. He waved his hand, motioning wildly for them to pull over.

"Okay," Trisha shouted. "This is where we get off. Hold on. Let's see if we can lose him on the turn!"

Trisha hit the gas and spun the wheel. Josh was thrown to the side as the van swerved onto the shoulder—and swung onto a side road.

A two-lane highway.

"Way to go, Trisha!" Deirdre shouted.

"Yeah! Eat our dust, cowboy!" Josh gazed back . . .

And cursed. The black car screeched, then roared onto the highway behind them.

"No good!" he told Trisha. "He made the turn. He's still dogging us."

And the two-lane highway was narrow. The roadway ahead snaked and curved.

This was a totally different driving game.

Tromping on the gas, Trisha tried to lose him. She muscled the van around a sharp curve. Then she floored the gas pedal through a straight stretch of road.

But it was useless. The black car stayed on their trail, nosing up to their bumper.

Josh heard the engine rev behind him.

Now what? he wondered, twisting back.

The driver darted across the double yellow line. . . . into the opposite lane!

"Does that jerk have a death wish?" Mickey cried.

The black car roared up beside them.

"Pull over!" the cowboy growled. "Do it! Now!"

As he yelled, he yanked his wheel to the right. The fender of his car banged into the side of the van.

The sound of scraping metal made Josh's stomach lurch.

Frantically Trisha maneuvered the wheel.

The speedometer read 90.

Josh squeezed his eyes shut.

If they collided at this speed, the two vehicles would spin like tops.

We could be crushed! he thought.

"Back off!" Gary shouted at the psycho driver.

But the cowboy hunkered down and hit the gas. A total maniac.

Then something on the highway ahead caught Josh's eye. An enormous truck emerged from the bend in the road.

No time to slow down. Now way to swerve.

Josh moaned in horror.

This is it, he thought. I'm going to die in a car crash.

He gripped the armrest—and braced himself for the awful impact.

Chapter Four

A Deadly Surprise

Josh tightly shut his eyes.

He heard the roar of the truck.

Horns blaring.

The squeal of brakes.

The terrified cries of his friends.

He opened his eyes in time to see the black convertible shoot ahead of them in a crazy zigzag.

It swerved past the truck. Just missed. Just missed! And plunged off the road into the desert.

Josh gasped for air. He realized he hadn't been breathing!

The truck sped by. The driver glared at them angrily, hit the horn twice, then moved on.

The van had come to a dead stop. And everyone seemed okay. Stunned, but unhurt.

His heart thudding in his chest, Josh

17

peered out. The cowboy's car had spun to a stop, wedged against a barrel cactus. Its tires were buried in sand. Spinning furiously. Digging deeper, until the car was buried up to its chassis.

Trisha rested her face against the wheel. "I'm still shaking," she whispered.

"You're not the only one," Josh told her. He raked his hair back and rubbed the knees of his jeans. "Is everyone okay?"

"I—I . . ." Deirdre's voice quivered. "I thought we were dead."

Josh glanced over at the black convertible. The angry cowboy pushed on the door, then climbed out over it to inspect the damage.

"Looks like he's okay," Josh muttered.

"Yeah, but he's stuck," Gary said. "His car doesn't have four-wheel drive. It'll take a tow truck to drag him out of the sand."

"Good," Trisha said. "That gives us plenty of time to get out of here." She took a long, deep breath, then braced herself against the steering wheel.

"Trisha, do you want me to drive?" Mickey offered.

"That's okay." Trisha sighed. Then she grabbed the gearshift. "We're not far from the ranch. And I know the way."

As they cruised down the highway, Josh tried to relax. But all his muscles were tight and tense. His head spun.

No one talked.

Josh started to feel better when he spotted

a carved wooden sign: HOHOKAM RANCH, NEXT RIGHT.

They swung off the main road, under an arched gate that marked the entrance.

Tension drained away as the ranch came into view.

They cruised down a lane lined with palm trees to the sprawling complex of low, clay-colored buildings with sparkling windows and red-tiled roofs.

Josh blinked. He'd expected dry sandy desert. Instead he saw emerald green lawns and climbing vines with colorful blossoms. And that scent—orange trees?

To the right, horses grazed outside a barn.

To the left, water sparkled in several aquamarine swimming pools. Beyond the pools, he saw two shady gazebos and a tennis court.

Josh flashed Mickey a grin. "Think you can deal with this place?"

Mickey gave him a thumbs-up. "Not too shabby."

Trisha pulled up in front of the main house and jumped to the ground. "I'm totally wrecked." She sighed.

"I think we all are," Deirdre replied. "But we made it in one piece! Awesome driving!" She swung a hand around Trisha's shoulders.

Gary hopped out and circled the vehicle. "The fender is okay. But look at this. That creep scratched the paint!"

Josh gathered with his friends around the dented panel. He was trailing his fingers over

19

the scratch when a man pushed open the screen door and joined the group.

"What happened, Trisha?" he asked. His long black hair was tied back under a straw Stetson.

"Oh, Simon, it was awful!" Trisha groaned. She introduced the kids to the ranch foreman, Simon Travis. Then she told Simon about the crazy lunatic cowboy.

"I'm grateful none of you was hurt," Simon said softly.

Josh nodded. The foreman seemed really nice.

"I'd better get this vehicle off to the mechanic," Simon told them. "I'll drop your luggage off at the west patio, closer to your rooms." He jumped in and drove off.

Trisha pushed her blond hair back and asked, "You guys want to hit the pool?"

"Sounds like a plan," Gary said. "An excellent plan."

"Your rooms are in the west wing," Trisha said, pointing to the wing of the house that stretched near the sparkling pools. "Follow me if you want the tour—and some lemonade."

As they cut across the green lawn, Trisha pointed out the buildings housing the gym, the game room with computer games and Ping-Pong tables, and the main dining hall. "There's usually someone around if you get hungry," she said.

Josh tried not to gape. He knew that the Conrads were loaded, but he didn't expect the ranch to be so luxurious.

Trisha held open a screen door, and they filed into an atrium. The floor was a patchwork of stone and gardens with exotic flowers and cacti.

"This is the main patio," Trisha announced.

"And here's our stuff." Gary pulled out his backpack, and two other bags rolled to the stone floor.

One of them belonged to Josh.

He groaned as the side pocket of his bag flew open and clothes started to spill out.

Just then a girl appeared. About their age. Beautiful, with shiny black hair and wide green eyes.

She is *hot*! Josh thought. He quickly pushed the clothes back into his bag.

Gary grinned. "Last one in the pool is a dead man."

"That's not funny," Deirdre said, hoisting her suitcases. "Not after our near disaster getting here!"

"Don't forget this." The black-haired girl handed Josh a can of shaving cream. "It must have rolled under the hammock."

He took the can and shoved it into his bag without looking. He couldn't take his eyes off her deep green eyes.

Josh felt his face get hot. This girl could be a model, he thought. Or a movie star!

"Thanks." He straightened up. "Guess I'm the fastest klutz in the West."

She smiled, flashing perfect white teeth.

"I'm Josh," he said, with an awkward smile.

"We're Trisha's friends." He studied her. She was probably eighteen or nineteen. Did she work here part-time?

"I know." She smiled. "I know everything about the Hohokam Ranch. My father is the foreman."

Simon's daughter? Josh could see the resemblance. They had the same black hair and slight build. "So you've lived here—"

"All my life," the girl answered. "I was here before the Conrads bought the place and—"

"Excuse me, Rose," Trisha cut in. "Could you do me a favor? Could you get one of the hands in here and make sure all the bags get to their rooms?"

Rose's smile faded. "Of course."

"If you could do it *now* . . ." Trisha said.

Surprised, Josh turned toward Trisha. It wasn't like her to order people around.

But there was something brewing between the girls—

A flicker of tension. Resentment?

He wasn't sure. But Rose was already gone. And Trisha, arm-in-arm with Gary, led Josh and Deirdre through the open corridor, shaded by flowering vines.

Josh closed up the flap on his bag and caught up with the others.

"You're sharing with Mickey," Trisha said, steering Josh into a large room. A stone fireplace filled one wall. Rough-hewn beams lined the ceiling. The floors were pale, polished wood.

"See you at the pool," Deirdre called from the hallway.

Closing the door, Josh felt as if he had stepped into an old cowboy movie.

Mickey heaved his bag onto the bed by the window. "Can you believe this place? We've scored. Big time."

"I should have brought my tennis racket," Josh said, unzipping his duffel bag.

"I'm sure Trisha can loan you one. Or two. And how about that Mercedes van? She almost wrecks this expensive set of wheels, and the foreman just drives it off to fix it."

"Yeah," Josh said. "My father would freak. Then he'd cash in my college fund."

He reached into the jumble of clothes for his swimsuit.

He pulled out a western shirt with shiny buttons. "Huh?" he gasped. "I don't have a shirt like that."

He lifted out a tooled leather belt. Not his. Red boxers with yellow smiley faces on them. Definitely not his.

"This isn't my stuff." Josh dug through the clothes.

His fingers closed around something cold and hard.

With a distinctive shape.

Josh gaped as he pulled it out.

Heavy and cold, it dangled in his hand . . .

A gun.

Chapter Five

House of Fear

"**W**hoa!" Mickey exclaimed. "Put that thing down. What if it's loaded?"

Josh lowered the pistol to the bed and stared down at it. From the round barrel he could see that it was a revolver. It was all shiny steel except for the butt of the gun, which was black, carved in a criss-cross pattern.

"I can't believe this!" Josh said.

"Yeah," Mickey agreed. "Weird enough that you get your bag switched with someone. But to end up with a gun . . ."

"A gun that was on a plane," Josh pointed out. "How'd this bag get past airport security?"

Josh shivered as he stared at the weapon.

What if the gun had been used to hurt someone. . . .

"Maybe it belongs to an FBI agent or something," Mickey suggested.

Josh nodded. "Yeah, right. There's got to be some ID in here."

Mickey pulled a wad of clothes out of the bag and pawed through them. Josh searched inside, shaking out jeans and T-shirts and shorts.

In the back pocket of one pair of jeans he felt something stiff. He slid out a photo ID from a Tucson gym. The square, beefy face and flat-top haircut were familiar.

Too familiar.

"It's him," Josh groaned. "The guy who nearly killed us."

Mickey snatched the card from Josh's hand. "Clay Hartley," he read. "One-five-two Sedona Drive. Here in Tucson." He handed the card back to Josh. "It's been nice knowing you, partner. He'll *kill* you when he finds out you took his bag!"

"But—don't you see?" Josh dropped onto the bed. "That's why he was chasing us! He knew we had his bag. That we'd find the gun . . ."

"And bang-bang, you're dead." Mickey frowned. "And right at the beginning of spring break. That's a shame."

Josh sighed. "I'm not laughing, okay?"

Mickey picked up the gun, weighing it in one hand. "Why do you think he has this? I mean, he didn't come off as the cop type."

"Who knows?" Josh jumbled up clothes and shoved them into the bag. "I don't *want* to know. I just want to give it back and get my clothes. No questions asked. Then I'll be done with cowboy what's-his-name."

"Clay Hartley," Mickey reminded him.

"Whatever." Josh rolled the revolver up in an orange T-shirt and carefully placed it in the bag.

"So give it back. *Later*," Mickey said, pulling on a T-shirt. "Do you want to borrow some swim trunks?"

Josh shook his head. "I want to get rid of this thing now. I can swim when I get back."

"Suit yourself." Mickey lowered his shades and headed off to the pool.

Josh lugged the bag back down the corridor. He found Simon in the west lobby. Rose stood off in a sunny corner, watering plants. The foreman hoisted a suitcase onto a cart and turned to Josh.

"My bag got snagged at the airport," Josh explained. "This one belongs to someone else."

"Hmm." Simon touched his chin. "We can call the airline. They'll probably send a van out tonight. Or early tomorrow."

The airline . . .

Josh gritted his teeth. They'd sort through the bag. Find the gun. Maybe even confiscate it. Clay wouldn't be too happy about that.

Josh shook his head. No way. He wasn't going to spend spring break looking over his shoulder, worried about Clay Hartley coming after him.

"I can't wait," Josh said. "I mean, I need my clothes and stuff. Can one of the ranch hands drive this out to the owner? Maybe make a switch?"

"I'm sorry," Simon answered. "But I can't spare anyone this afternoon." He wheeled the luggage cart out into the bright sunlight.

Thanks for nothing, Josh thought, discouraged.

"But you don't have any clothes, right?" Rose moved closer to check out the ID tag. "Sedona Drive . . . he lives near my friend." She smiled at Josh. "I'll drop it off."

She reached for the duffelbag, but Josh pulled it back.

"Wait a minute," he said. "This is the guy who smashed into us outside the airport. He's dangerous."

Rose shrugged. "Once he spots his bag, he won't be so dangerous."

Josh felt a tug of fear as he gazed into Rose's green eyes. He couldn't let her do this. Not alone.

"Okay," he agreed. "But I'm going with you."

Fifteen minutes later Rose slowed the small pickup truck. "This is Sedona Drive," she said, pointing to the right. "The house should be on that side of the road."

Josh counted ahead to one-five-two, to a small ranch house, hidden behind overgrown sagebrush and weeds. An old house. With a cracked porch and a sagging roof.

"It looks deserted," he said. "And sort of creepy."

Rose turned off the engine. "We'll check it out."

"You'd better wait here," Josh said. "This

guy is basically a psycho."

He pushed open his door and stepped out. "This probably won't take long."

Lugging the duffel bag up to the porch, he knocked on the door and waited.

No answer.

Josh knocked again, and the door gave way. It was open.

He gave the splintered wood a slight push . . .

Revealing the small living room. A cardboard box. Furniture covered with dusty cloths. An old mattress on the floor.

It felt empty. Too empty for anyone to be living here.

Was this Clay Hartley's *old* address? Had he moved away?

Maybe I should just leave the duffel bag, Josh thought. If he knew for sure that Clay would be back, he'd be happy to dump the bag—and the gun.

Maybe something in this room had Clay's name on it. A piece of mail or a magazine . . .

Gritting his teeth, Josh stepped into the room. His sneakers scraped on the dusty floor as he crossed to the cardboard box.

It wasn't sealed shut.

Bending down, Josh lifted one of the cardboard flaps.

A digital alarm clock sat on top of a mound of things wrapped in newspaper. Next he unwrapped a small lamp. Then a ceramic bowl.

This is useless, Josh thought as he dug out another item. There was no way of knowing if

Clay would find his bag here. Besides, this place was creepy. Stuffy and hot and dusty.

Wiping the beads of sweat from his upper lip, Josh heard the first noise. A strange, heavy rumble.

As if the house was moaning.

Too weird, he thought as the house grumbled again. Time to get out of here.

Josh reached for the duffel bag—and it slid away.

The floor was shuddering under his sneakers.

The walls groaned and shook—violently.

Josh struggled to stay on his feet. The entire house was rattling. . . .

Roaring . . .

Swallowing him!

Chapter Six

What is She Hiding?

What's going on?

No time to react.

The walls roared. The ground shook again.

Josh lost his balance. Tumbled to the dusty floor.

He forced himself shakily to his feet.

Take it easy, he thought. Slow, steady steps.

He reached out for something solid—the bookcase. The scarred, wood shelves rose to the ceiling. He grabbed the edge and the room rocked again.

The bookcase tipped. Falling toward him.

Josh gasped. He was going to be crushed!

With a loud cry, he dodged to the side.

It fell with a crash. One corner grazed his arm.

A cloud of dust shot up as the shelves crashed to the floor.

Crushed . . . he thought. I would have been crushed.

He grabbed the duffel bag and bolted out the door, violently choking as the sunlight hit him. Screaming. Shouting in panic.

"Josh!" Rose shouted through the open truck window. "Are you okay?"

He swallowed hard. Struggled to catch his breath. "Yeah . . . I guess." He yanked open the truck door and hoisted himself into the seat.

"That earthquake was pretty big," Rose said.

Earthquake?

Well, that explains that, Josh thought. An earthquake. And I ran out of there like a squawking chicken. Right in front of Rose.

She must think I'm a total wimp.

Talk about embarrassing.

"I think it was an aftershock," Rose said. "We had a pretty big one two days ago. Maybe that's the last of them."

"I hope . . ." Josh choked out.

"So . . . you decided not to leave that?" Rose nodded at the duffel bag, which Josh had stuffed onto the floor of the cab.

Josh shrugged. "The place looks abandoned. Like someone started packing, then just took off."

"What are you going to do?" she asked.

"I don't know. I guess I'll take it to the airport tomorrow or something. I can borrow some clothes from Mickey, but I need to hit a store."

"No problem," Rose said. "There's a mall on the way back to the ranch. Besides, I *love* shopping."

31

She kept glancing at him as they drove back to the ranch. Her eyes seemed to be questioning him. A couple of times she opened her mouth to speak, but then changed her mind.

Strange, Josh thought.

What is she thinking about? Why does she keep looking at me that way—as if she has some kind of secret, some kind of secret she can't bring herself to share?

PART TWO

"**Y**uck!" Josie Maxwell twisted her face in disgust. She raised her fingernails to Jennifer Fear, jiggling her fingers like spiderlegs.

"I hate this color," Josie declared. "Why'd you give me this color? What's it called? *Dried Blood*?"

Jennifer lowered her *People* magazine and studied Josie's glittering wet fingernails. "It's called *Grape Juice*," she replied. "What's wrong with it? I think it's hot."

"Hot?" Josie rolled her eyes. "I think it's ghoulish. It would look good on someone in the *Addams Family*! You know—jet-black hair, white face makeup, every body part pierced."

Jennifer laughed. "That might be a good new look for you." She went back to the *People* magazine. "Do you think Antonio Banderas is sexy?"

Josie frowned. "I don't *have* a look. That's my whole problem."

Jennifer shut the magazine and dropped it to the carpet. "Why can't we talk about Antonio Banderas?"

"Because we're talking about my nails," Josie whined.

They were sitting in Josie's bedroom. Josie hunched over the small, round table against the wall, gazing fretfully at her dark purple nails. Jennifer stretched out on the floor, her back against Josie's bed.

A square of warm, yellow sunlight washed over Jennifer from the open window. A warm breeze fluttered the curtain. The spring air smelled fresh and sweet.

Jennifer gazed up at her friend. "Would you say you're a little *gloomy*?"

Josie sneered back at her. "Do camels spit?"

Jennifer laughed. "What does *that* mean?"

"It means I'm gloomy," Josie snapped. "It means you and I are sitting here in Shadyside, as usual, with nothing to do for spring break. It means I'm sitting here wasting my time, making myself ugly, having no fun, no excitement of any kind. It means I'm—"

"Glad you're enjoying my company!" Jennifer interrupted. She pulled herself to her feet, tugging her T-shirt down over her denim cutoffs. "If you want me to go . . ."

"It's not *your* fault that we're bored out of our skulls!" Josie declared. "Tell me, Jen—why should my brother be out in Arizona having the time of his life while I'm sitting home watching *Loveline* on MTV?"

"Josie, stop—" Jennifer pleaded.

"Why should Dana and Josh, and Mickey, and Trisha be living it up on a fancy dude ranch, while we—"

"Didn't you hear?" Jennifer interrupted. "Dana couldn't go. She was sick. So Deirdre went instead."

Josie blinked, surprised. "Poor Dana," she murmured.

"Poor *Mickey*," Jennifer corrected her. "He was looking forward to a hot week alone with her." A sly smile spread over Jennifer's face. "I guess Deirdre will have to take her sister's place. She'll like that. Everyone knows she has a thing for Mickey."

Josie's expression grew thoughtful. She blew on her nails. Then she turned back to her friend. "You could have gone, Jen. Trisha invited you."

Jennifer sighed and dropped down onto the edge of the bed. "My stupid parents . . . " she murmured. "They're always in my face." Angry pink circles formed on her cheeks.

"I know, I know," Josie said. "Your parents wouldn't let you go. You told me the whole story. They're fed up with you."

Jennifer turned away from Josie and stared out the window. A car rolled by on the street, radio blaring rap music, guys singing along, shouting out of the car windows.

"But you never told me why you've been so

angry at your parents lately," Josie continued.

Jennifer didn't reply. She gazed out the window. When she turned back to Josie, her cheeks were still pink. "You know, something exciting could happen this spring break," she said, changing the subject.

"Like what?" Josie demanded.

"Like we could meet really cool guys somewhere. You never know. Or the phone could ring. And it could be some secret admirer, some guy who always wanted to call you. Some guy who's going to totally change your life."

Josie laughed. "Yeah, right."

And the phone rang.

Both girls gasped.

"See?" Jennifer said, grinning. "Go ahead. Pick it up."

Josie hesitated. The phone rang again.

She grabbed it and raised it to her ear. "Hello?"

Chapter Eight

Let's Do Something Dangerous

When Josie heard the voice on the other end of the line, she burst out laughing. The phone fell out of her hand and clattered onto the table. Josie tossed her head back and laughed.

Jennifer jumped up from the bed and hurried across the room. She grabbed the edge of the table. "What's so funny? *What?*"

"It's . . . Josh!" Josie managed to choke out.

Now both girls laughed.

Josie could hear Josh's tinny shouts in the phone.

Wiping a tear off her cheek, she raised the phone back to her ear. "No. I can't tell you what's so funny," she told her brother. "No. I can't tell you. You wouldn't get it."

Still laughing, Jennifer smoothed back her straight dark hair. She pulled out a chair and sat across from Josie.

"Jen's here. We're not doing anything," Josie sighed into the phone. "What are *you* doing? Calling me? Yes, I *know* you're calling me."

Jennifer shook her head. "Josh thinks he's so funny," she murmured to Josie.

"So how's it going?" Josie demanded. "How is the fabulous ranch? How is the fabulous Trisha?" She listened. Her expression changed. "You *what*? A drunken cowboy? You got into a fight?"

Jennifer's mouth dropped open. "That doesn't sound like Josh."

Josie motioned for her to be quiet. "You're okay?" she asked into the phone. "Who started the fight? *You* didn't—right? Yeah . . . yeah . . . ? Well . . . *that's* disturbing."

Josie stood up and started to pace the small room. "No. Mom and Dad aren't home. They're shopping or something. Why'd you call? Because they told you to call? Okay. I'll tell them. No—I *won't* tell them about the fight. Promise. So . . . it's great there, huh? Yeah. Okay. Okay. You've got to go. What am I doing? Not much. Just hanging out. You know. Okay. Have fun. Bye."

Josie clicked the phone off. She stared at it a moment before she turned to Jennifer. "He's having a great time."

Jennifer nodded. "Cool." She grinned. "Does he know any drunken cowboys for *us*?"

Josie tossed the phone to the bed. "These nails are really gross." She sighed. "I can't go outside with these. I—"

"Josh gave me an idea," Jennifer interrupted. Her eyes flashed excitedly. "You want to do something tonight?"

Josie rolled her eyes. "I'll check my calendar and see if I can fit you in!"

"I just remembered something I have," Jennifer replied, ignoring the sarcasm. "Something I hid away for the perfect occasion."

Josie studied her friend. "I'm starting to get interested. What exactly are we talking about here?"

"You'll see," Jennifer said mysteriously. She picked up her bag and started to the door. "I'll pick you up around nine. Wear something sexy. Something a little outrageous. But sophisticated. Try to look older."

Josie blinked. "Why? Come on, Jen—where are we going? Tell me. What are we doing?"

Jennifer smiled. "Something dangerous."

Chapter Nine

Jail Bait

At ten after nine Josie heard a car horn honking in the driveway. "That's Jen," she told her parents. "See you later."

"Not too late!" her mother called.

Why don't you tattoo those words on your forehead? Josie thought, frowning. Then you wouldn't have to say them *every single night I go out*!

She checked herself in the front hall mirror. She had a silky, sleeveless purple top tucked into a short black skirt. The purple top almost matched her nails. She had pulled on lots of jewelry, long, clicking, yellow plastic earrings, about a dozen plastic bracelets.

"Not bad," she murmured.

She hurried out to the car.

"Hey." Josie slid into the passenger seat and studied her friend. Jennifer was dressed in black, a black shirt over a black T-shirt, tight black slacks. She had her hair piled up on her head.

"Wow. I like the eye makeup!" Josie told her. "Very dramatic! You look about twenty-five."

"That's the idea," Jennifer replied mysteriously. She checked Josie out. "Very slinky." Then she backed down the driveway.

Josie pulled the seatbelt over her chest. "Well . . . I'm ready for adventure. Where are we going?"

Jennifer turned the radio up but didn't reply. She turned the car onto Canyon Drive.

"So? Where are the guys?" Josie asked. "Where is the excitement?"

"It's a surprise," Jennifer replied, her eyes flashing mischievously.

"You know I hate surprises," Josie declared. "Come on. You're making me really nervous. Tell me, Jen. Where are we going?"

Jennifer sighed. She turned onto the highway. "Okay. The Roadhouse."

"The *what*?"

"The Roadhouse," Jennifer repeated. "You know. Right outside Waynesbridge."

"A bar?" Josie cried. "That's the idea you got from Josh? Oh, I get it. The drunken cowboy. What do you want to do? Sit in a bar and—and get *wrecked*?"

Jennifer laughed. "Well . . . it'd be *different*."

"No. Really—" Josie insisted.

"My idea is we'll meet older guys," Jennifer told her, passing a slow-moving van. "A lot

43

of guys from the college hang out at the Roadhouse, right?"

"Well . . . yeah," Josie agreed. "Because you have to be twenty-one."

"Right. So it won't be filled with a lot of high school geeks," Jennifer explained. "It'll be great. We'll meet some hot older guys."

Josie groaned. "Aren't you forgetting one little thing?" she cried shrilly. "We're not twenty-one. We're eighteen, Jennifer! We are high school geeks, too. There's no way we're getting into the Roadhouse."

A smug, all-knowing smile spread over Jennifer's face. Her eyes, dark and dramatic from the heavy mascara, flashed almost gleefully.

"Well—?" Josie demanded.

"That's what I remembered I have," Jennifer said, turning onto the Waynesbridge exit. "Hidden in the back of my dresser drawer."

"What? *What?*"

"Fake ID, of course."

Josie narrowed her eyes at her grinning friend. "Excuse me?"

"I have fake I.D. cards. For both of us."

"Where'd you get them?"

"Deirdre had them made," Jennifer replied, slowing for a light. "When school started last fall. One for her and one for me. I've never used mine, but—"

"Whoa. Wait a minute," Josie said. "You mean—I have to use Deirdre's card?"

Jennifer nodded.

"But—but—" Josie sputtered. "I don't look anything like Deirdre! She's blonde! And she—she—"

"Okay. So it's not a perfect plan," Jennifer confessed.

A pink and blue neon sign rose over the narrow road, blinking the word ROADHOUSE on and off. Jennifer turned sharply into the gravel parking lot.

The car bounced closer to a long, low shingled building that looked more like a shack than a restaurant. The headlights rolled over a couple dressed all in denim, leaning against the back wall, making out.

Two guys sat on the hood of a car, drinking beer from dark bottles. Latin salsa music blared from the open door of the bar.

"This isn't going to work," Josie protested. She suddenly had a heavy feeling in the pit of her stomach.

"Of course it is," Jennifer replied, cutting the engine. "The bar is really dark, right? So you flash the ID card fast. No one will be able to see the photo."

She clicked off the headlights. "Besides, no one will even ask. You know how these places are."

"No, I don't," Josie murmured.

She climbed out of the car. The night air felt cool and damp. The heavy, slightly sour aroma of beer floated from the bar.

"Try not to look so terrified," Jennifer said, tucking the car keys into her bag. "Bartenders can smell fear."

Josie frowned.

"Hey—that was a joke!" Jennifer cried. "Come on, what's your problem? We're going to have some adventure, right? We're going to meet some hot guys. What's the worst thing that could happen?"

"Well . . . there could be an off-duty cop in the bar," Josie replied. "He could arrest us. Take us to the station. Our parents would have to come get us. And that would be the end of spring break."

"No way!" Jennifer declared. "No way. I had no idea you were such a worrier, Josie."

"Yes, you did," Josie murmured.

Making their way past the denim couple, who were wrapped around each other, lip-locked against the wall, they stepped up to the open front door. Josie heard blaring music. Laughing voices. The soft clatter of glasses and bottles. The *clack* of billiard balls.

No one was posted at the entrance. No one checked ID's.

Josie crossed her fingers and followed Jennifer inside.

The heavy alcohol aroma, the smoke-filled air nearly took her breath away. She stopped in front of the crowded bar, blinking, waiting for her eyes to adjust to the dim light.

"I don't see any tables!" Jennifer shouted over the loud voices and booming jukebox. "But there sure are a lot of guys!"

Josie jumped, startled, as a young guy behind her let out a loud WHOOP! He started wrestling playfully with the guy beside him. People laughed and cheered him on.

"Over here," Jennifer said, tugging Josie's arm. Two stools at the bar had opened up. Jennifer dived for them, claiming them just in front of two college girls who had the same idea.

Josie slid onto the stool beside her. "Nice move!" she exclaimed, flashing Jennifer a thumbs-up. She arranged her small bag on her lap and looked around.

She could see only one bartender, way at the other end of the bar. He was a good-looking guy, probably a college student, with wavy blond hair and a nice smile.

The crowd down there was about three deep, Josie saw. The bartender was scribbling orders rapidly, wiping sweat off his forehead with the sleeve of his white shirt.

"What do you want to drink?" Jennifer asked. "I'm going to have a beer. All those college guys over there are drinking beers."

Josie started to answer—but stopped with her mouth open. The bartender had asked for a girl's ID. Josie watched as the girl handed it to him. He raised it to his face and studied it carefully.

"Let's go," Josie urged. "This isn't going to work."

Jennifer had the two false ID cards in her hand. "Will you give me a break?" she said impatiently. "It's going to be fine."

"But he's looking at her card!" Josie

protested, pointing down the bar.

"Let me order," Jennifer suggested, patting Josie's hand. "I look older than you. Maybe he'll only look at my ID."

"Maybe . . ." Josie murmured.

"The main thing is to smile," Jennifer scolded. "A sweet, confident, twenty-one-year-old smile."

"Okay. I'll try," Josie replied. She gripped the edge of the wooden bar with both hands. "Here he comes. Good luck!"

The bartender stopped to talk to a young woman with long, white-blond hair. Then he began to make his way to Josie's end of the bar.

He was still several stools away—when Josie felt a hand grab her shoulder roughly from behind.

And a deep voice boomed, *"You're both under arrest. Come with me."*

Chapter Ten

What a Night!

Josie uttered a cry.

The hand dug into her shoulder.

"Hey—whoa!" She heard Jennifer's startled cry.

Her heart thudded. Josie swallowed hard. Felt dizzy.

Caught . . . caught!

She spun around—and stared into the grinning face of Matty Winger.

Matty Winger, Shadyside senior. Voted Most Likely to Be a Nerd for the Rest of His Life.

"Gotcha both," Matty said gleefully, very pleased with the frightened cries he had provoked. "What are you two doing here?"

Jennifer regained her voice first. "What are *you* doing here?" she choked out.

Josie couldn't stop her heart from racing.

Matty Winger. Of all people. Yuck.

Was this the low point of her life?

Well . . . the night was still young.

"I've got a table," Matty told Jennifer, grinning proudly. When he smiled, he looked like Beaver on that goofy old TV show.

"Can you get us some beers?" Jennifer asked.

"Yeah. Sure. No problem," he replied, patting her shoulder. "Hey, Jen—I like the new look."

"Thanks for noticing," Jennifer said sarcastically. "You made my night."

Matty laughed. He had never understood sarcasm. "Come on." He pulled them off their bar stools. "I want you to meet somebody."

He dragged them to a small wooden booth near the back, big enough for only two people. "Come on. Squeeze in," he urged.

A guy about their age, with a crooked smile and a buzz cut that ended in a tiny rat tail, leaned out at them. He had a skinny face, tiny, round eyes, and big lips. He reminded Josie of a ferret someone brought to school once.

"Meet my cousin!" Matty declared proudly. "Come on. Scoot in. There's room for everybody. Mo, this is Josie and Jennifer. From my school."

Josie nodded to the ferret. "Hi."

Jennifer leaned over the booth. "Mo? Your name is Mo? Mo Winger?"

He nodded. His Adam's apple bobbed up and down in his slender throat.

"What's Mo short for?" Jennifer asked.

50

"It's short for Mo," Matty's cousin replied. He wasn't joking.

Jennifer brought her face close to Josie's and whispered, "See? I told you we'd meet some cool guys."

Josie tromped down hard on Jennifer's foot.

Matty slid into the booth across from his cousin. "Come on. Don't stand there. Slide in," he urged the girls.

"Want to go?" Jennifer whispered to Josie.

Before Josie could answer, a waitress in a checked uniform and white apron stepped up to the booth. "What can I get you guys?"

"I'm buying," Matty declared, pulling out his battered wallet and slapping it down on the table. "I'm buying for everybody."

"Well, what'll it be?" the waitress asked.

"Uh . . . do you have shooters?" Matty asked.

The waitress narrowed her eyes at him. "I'll have to see your ID," she said. She held out her hand.

Matty thumped his wallet on the table. "Well . . . I forgot it, actually. But I'm a student, see. At Waynesbridge Junior College. You know. So . . ."

"I really have to see ID," the waitress insisted patiently.

"I just forgot it," Matty repeated. "But I'm twenty-one. Really. You can probably tell, right?"

The waitress waved to a large, powerful-looking guy in tight jeans and a muscle shirt. He nodded and began lumbering toward them, flexing his biceps.

"Good night, folks," the waitress said pleasantly.

A few seconds later the four Shadyside seniors were standing in the gravel parking lot. "Sorry," Matty apologized, shaking his head. "I thought I could convince her."

"You should have slipped her five dollars," Mo suggested. "Then I bet she'd let us stay." He opened his mouth in a high-pitched laugh, as if he'd said something funny.

Josie let out a long sigh. Partly from relief. Partly from unhappiness at how the big, adventurous night was working out. "Guess we'd better go," she said, glancing at Jennifer.

"No. Wait," Matty urged. "It's still early, right? Why don't we go somewhere? You could come with Mo and me."

"I—I don't think so," Josie stammered.

"We could . . . uh . . . drive up to the river," Matty suggested. A devilish grin spread over his round face. "We could fool around or something." Then he whispered, loud enough for both girls to hear, "My cousin has never made out with a girl."

"Now *that's* a surprise!" Jennifer said, rolling her eyes.

She and Josie both burst out laughing.

They were still laughing a few minutes later, wiping tears from their eyes, as Matty and Mo drove away.

"Wow. What a night," Josie murmured finally.

"I guess this was better than being poked with a sharp stick," Jennifer said.

"I think I'd like to try the stick," Josie replied.

And they both started laughing again.

They laughed until they saw Jennifer's car.

Josie noticed it first. It sat at an odd angle. Slanted to one side.

It didn't take them long to realize that a back tire was flat.

"Oh, great," Jennifer muttered. "This is just perfect. I flunked driver's ed. I don't know how to change a stupid tire."

As if on cue, two guys appeared from around a blue van.

"Need some help?" the taller one asked, his eyes moving from the tire to the girls.

"Want us to change it?" his friend asked.

"Would you?" Jennifer replied. "That would really be great."

And that's when the trouble began.

Chapter **Eleven**

"Made You Scream, Right?"

Josie helped Jennifer pull the jack and tire tools from the truck. The two guys introduced themselves. Tim and Evan.

"You can wait in our van if you want," Tim said, pointing to the blue van behind them. "This won't take long."

"Cool van," Jennifer murmured. Josie followed her to the side of the van as the guys started to work.

"Which is which?" Josie whispered.

Jennifer gazed at them. "I think the tall, skinny one with the baseball cap and the great eyes is Tim. The shorter one with the great bod and the wicked smile is Evan."

The boys talked and laughed as they worked. Josie watched them pull the flat tire off and carry it to Jennifer's trunk.

Jennifer leaned back against the side of the

54

van. "I'll take Evan," she told Josie. "He's short but he's choice."

Josie laughed. "What makes you think they're interested in us?"

"You'll see."

Josie watched Tim squatting beside the car, fitting the spare tire into place. Evan lay half under the car, helping his friend with the tire.

Josie turned to Jennifer. "Handy guys to have around," she said, grinning. "Maybe tonight will—"

Evan's shrill scream interrupted her.

"Ohhhh . . . help," he groaned. "Please . . . The jack . . . slipped. My legs . . . crushed . . ."

Josie and Jennifer both uttered horrified cries.

Josie turned—and saw Tim on his knees beside the tire, Evan still on the ground grinning up at them. Both boys burst out laughing.

"That wasn't funny!" Jennifer declared angrily, storming toward them.

Evan climbed to his feet, brushed off the front of his faded jeans. "Sure, it was," he replied, still grinning. "Made you scream, right?"

Josie's heart was still pounding. "You have a sick sense of humor," she said.

"That's what everyone tells us!" Tim replied. He motioned to the tire. "All fixed. You're ready to roll." He tossed the jack into Jennifer's trunk and slammed the lid.

Jennifer moved closer to them, brushing her hair back off her shoulders. "That was really nice of you," she said softly.

Tim pulled off his baseball cap and mopped his forehead with the sleeve of his Phish T-shirt. "Well, we saw you before in the bar," he said. "And we thought we'd like to meet you. That's why we let the air out of your tire."

Josie and Jennifer laughed. But Josie began to feel a little uncomfortable. "You're joking again—right?" she asked.

"Right!" they both answered in unison.

Are they kidding or not? Josie wondered. They didn't really give us a flat tire—did they?

She scolded herself for always being so cautious, so suspicious. *Don't spoil this*, she instructed herself.

"You guys go to Waynesbridge?" Jennifer asked.

"Excuse me?" Tim replied, wiping grease off his hands.

"You know. The college. You go to college?" Jennifer repeated.

"Oh, yeah. Right," Evan replied, grinning. He exchanged a quick glance with Tim. "Yeah. We go to college."

"Every day," Tim added. "We never miss a day."

Jennifer eyed them suspiciously. "What's your major?"

The two guys exchanged another glance. "Well . . . I'm majoring in flower arranging," Evan said. "And Tim is into modern dance."

They both burst out laughing. They slapped each other a high five.

"Do you do a stand-up act or something?" Jennifer demanded.

"Very funny," Josie muttered.

"No. Really. We're college students," Tim insisted. He shifted the cap on his head. "We're just goofing with you."

"We don't take ourselves too seriously," Evan added.

"We hadn't noticed," Jennifer replied dryly.

"You want to go somewhere?" Evan asked, shoving his hands in his jeans pockets. "Want to drive around or something?"

"Well . . ." Josie hesitated.

"There's a party we were going to. A dorm party," Tim said, his expression serious now, his eyes on Josie. "We could just stop by for a little while."

"Well . . . maybe for a little while," Jennifer replied.

Josie tugged her arm. "Could we talk for just a sec?" She pulled Jennifer around to the other side of the van.

"What do you think?" Jennifer asked. "I think Tim really likes you."

"Are we *really* going to go with them?" Josie whispered. "We don't *know* them!"

Jennifer frowned at her. "That was the point."

"But—but—" Josie sputtered. "They seem kind of strange. I mean, all the jokes."

"They're just goofing," Jennifer replied. "I think they're funny."

"But—but—"

"Would you rather hang out with Matty and Mo?" Jennifer demanded impatiently.

Josie glanced through the van windows at Evan and Tim. "Well . . . okay," she agreed.

If she wasn't so jealous of her brother Josh out in Arizona . . .

If she wasn't so totally bored . . .

If they hadn't run into Matty Winger and his ferret cousin . . .

Josie never would have agreed to go with these two guys. She thought they seemed . . . dangerous. A little twisted.

Or was she just being timid and afraid as always?

Their shoes crunched over the gravel as they returned to the boys. "Let's check out the party," Jennifer said.

"But we can't stay too late," Josie added.

"Great!" Evan replied. "We'll go in the van, okay? Then Tim and I will bring you back to your car after the party."

"Well . . . let me get it started first," Tim said, trotting to the driver's side. "I've been having problems with the ignition." He climbed in.

They watched him leaning over the wheel. Silence. Then the van rumbled to life.

Josie climbed in front beside Tim. Jennifer scooted close to Evan in the seat behind them.

The tires skidded on the gravel. The neon ROADHOUSE sign blinked over the windshield. Then Tim lowered his foot on the gas pedal, and the van roared onto the road.

A row of darkened stores whirred by. Then

several blocks of small houses and mobile homes.

"So do you two live in Waynesbridge?" Tim asked as the van bounced over a hole in the road.

"No. Shadyside," Josie told him.

"You work or something?" Tim asked.

"We go to Shadyside High," Jennifer replied. "We're seniors."

"Awesome," Tim said. Josie caught him glancing at Evan in the rearview mirror.

The van rolled onto the highway.

"Whoa. Wait a minute!" Josie cried. "The college is back that way!"

"Really? I made a wrong turn," Tim said, his eyes on the road. "I meant to go the other way."

How fast were they going? Josie wondered. She glanced at the glowing speedometer. Eighty-five.

"Maybe we should just cruise around or something," Evan suggested. "Forget the party."

"No. Wait—" Josie started.

Then she heard the siren, a high shrill wail, coming up fast behind them.

She saw Tim's eyes go to the mirror. Caught the sudden look of fear on his face.

"Oh, wow," Tim murmured. "Oh, wow."

"What's wrong?" Jennifer demanded from behind them. "Why are they chasing us?"

"Well . . ." Tim replied slowly. "This van isn't exactly mine. We kinda . . . *borrowed* it."

Twelve

Wanna Play?

Josie shut her eyes. I don't believe this! she thought. Caught in a stolen van with two guys I've never seen before.

She pictured a dreary police station. Calling her parents to come get her. The tears . . . the shouting . . .

But then the siren wailed right by them. She opened her eyes. And watched the back of the squad car speed away.

"They—they weren't after us!" Josie declared happily.

Tim tossed back his head and laughed.

"What's up, guys?" Jennifer asked sternly. "Was that just another joke about stealing this van? Is it your van or not?"

"What do *you* think?" Evan replied.

The siren was faint in the distance now. Flat farmland rolled by the window, silvery under a bright half-moon.

"Of course it's my van," Tim said, grinning. "You girls scare easy! Are you sure you're seniors?"

"Are we going to this party or not?" Josie demanded.

"What party?" Evan replied.

"You're not funny," Jennifer told them. "Really."

"We try to have fun," Tim said, pretending to be hurt. "You don't have to be so cold. We have feelings, too, you know."

"Turn around," Evan instructed his friend. "Enough kidding around. Let's check out the dorm party."

Tim obediently turned the van around. They talked and laughed as they headed toward the campus. Josie started to feel more comfortable.

They're not so bad, she thought. They *are* kind of funny, actually. A lot more interesting than the boring high school geeks we hang out with.

And they seem to like us. . . .

She let herself go, laughed and joked with them. Tim is really cute, she decided. College guys are just so much more mature and interesting.

Josie's warm feelings faded as the van pulled up to the dorm on the Waynesbridge campus. Gazing out the van window at the dark, empty dorm lobby, a cold feeling swept over her.

Two couples stood beside the glass door talking. A man sat reading a newspaper at the lobby desk.

No one else around. No music. No dancing . . .

"Where's the party?" Josie asked.

Tim shrugged. "Guess it was canceled or something."

"Maybe we got the night wrong," Evan suggested. "Maybe it was last night."

"Maybe it was *never*," Jennifer snapped. "Could we go back to our car now?"

"You think we made it up?" Evan asked. "Give us a break! We made a mistake!"

"We weren't lying," Tim insisted, gazing intensely at Josie. "We're nice guys. Really. We changed your tire—right?"

"Want to get something to eat?" Evan suggested. "Why don't you come to our apartment? We'll order a pizza. We'll have our own party."

"Uh . . . I don't think so," Josie stammered. This was happening too fast. Were they good guys? Or were they creeps?

"Some other time, guys," Jennifer said. "Take us to our car, okay?"

"Some other time? Like tomorrow night?" Tim asked, his eyes still locked on Josie's.

"Maybe," Josie said. "I'll have to check."

"The four of us—we'll go out tomorrow night," Evan said, as if it had been decided. "Excellent."

Tim pulled the van away from the dorm and back onto the highway that led to the Roadhouse. Josie watched the road warily until she was sure he really was taking them back to the car.

I've got to stop being such a worrier, she decided.

Why can't I just stay loose? Go with it?

"Whatever."

I've got to learn to say "whatever."

Whatever happens. It's cool. Whatever.

Why can't I ever relax and say that?

The van crunched over the gravel of the Roadhouse parking lot. Jennifer wrote down their phone numbers on a little pad and handed them to Evan and Tim.

"How about giving us your number?" Josie asked.

"Well, here's the number. . . ." Tim cleared his throat. "We just moved into a new apartment. Our phone isn't hooked up yet."

Josie and Jennifer climbed out of the van. They waved to the guys as the van pulled away.

"Wow," Jennifer murmured.

Josie wasn't sure what she meant by that.

But she didn't get a chance to ask.

She saw Jennifer's expression change. Saw Jennifer's mouth drop open in shock.

And then Josie saw what had made Jennifer gasp. She saw the windshield of Jennifer's car. Saw the smears of red paint running down the glass, onto the hood. And then Josie saw that the paint spelled out two words:

WANNA PLAY?

PART THREE

Chapter Thirteen

The Vanished Ones

Josh pulled a sweatshirt over his head and followed Mickey out the door of their room. Once the sun went down, the desert cooled off. A nice break from the hot day. Good thing Mickey had packed an extra sweatshirt.

"We're meeting at the barbecue pit," Mickey told Josh. "It's just beyond the east wing."

They cut out through the west patio. Across the darkening lawn, Josh saw the fire. A dancing blaze in the center of a stonework barbecue.

A few rustic tables and benches were set with red-checkered tablecloths and napkins. Deirdre and Trisha sat at one table, eating big bowls of fruit salad.

Across from them a tall guy slouched over the table. His thick, dark hair curled over the collar of his denim jacket.

He made a comment that Josh couldn't hear. The girls exchanged a glance and laughed.

"Hey, wait up," Gary called, falling into step beside them.

"Who's that?" Josh asked.

"Roberto. He's some college guy," Mickey answered. "He's working on a dig on the other end of the ranch. Looking for artifacts and junk."

"Cool." Josh had always been interested in archaeology.

"Yeah. Cool—if you like dust and bones," Gary muttered. "Did you see the way he was coming on to Trisha at the pool?"

"So . . . what else did I miss?" Josh asked. He'd missed the action by the pool. By the time he and Rose got back from the mall, the sun was sliding down below the mountains.

"Why is he here, anyway?" Gary asked, ignoring Josh's question.

"He works part-time on the ranch," Mickey said.

"Well, somebody should clue him in about Trisha and me," Gary said, his eyes burning with anger.

"Whoa." Josh grinned, watching Roberto and the girls at the table. "Are you sure Trisha isn't coming on to *him*?"

Gary glared at Josh, then strode up to the table, where Roberto was holding court.

"College is great." Roberto was saying. "So you guys are all heading off next year. You're all seniors, right?"

Gary grabbed Trisha by the hand and pulled her up from the table.

"Yeah. We've all been through the college thing this year," Trisha told Roberto. She swung around to face Gary. "What's wrong?"

"You tell me," Gary muttered, glancing back at Roberto. "You said you'd wait for me in the west atrium, or whatever you call it."

"Oh. Sorry." Trisha squeezed his hand. "Deirdre and I were waiting for you. But then Roberto came along, and we figured we might as well . . ."

Josh watched them walk away. Then he followed Mickey to the main table covered with dishes. Potato salad, fruit salad, beans, rolls, chips . . .

"Chicken or ribs?" Simon called from the grill.

Josh and Mickey filled their plates and chowed down. Josh was tearing into a sparerib when he spotted Rose across the lawn. She carried a tray of brownies.

"Help yourself, guys," she said, holding the tray in front of Mickey and Josh.

"Whoa!" Josh wiped sauce from his chin and grabbed two brownies. "Did you bake these?"

Rose rolled her eyes. "Sure. And I milked the cows and grew the corn and plucked the chickens, too."

Mickey laughed, and Josh wanted to crawl under the table.

Why do I always act so lame around Rose? Every time he saw her, he turned into a super geek.

Simon pulled the metal grills off of the barbecue pit and added more wood. The guys moved the benches. Trisha and Deirdre spread out two blankets, and everyone gathered around the huge bonfire.

When Rose slid onto the bench beside him, Josh felt a little better. Okay, time to relax. No more stupid comments.

"This is so awesome." Deirdre sighed. "I feel a million miles away from Shadyside. What a great dinner!" She dropped onto a blanket near the fire.

"The big barbecue. It's a Hohokam Ranch tradition," Simon said proudly.

"Hey, how come it's not called the Conrad Ranch?" Gary asked.

"We could call it that," Trisha said, linking her fingers through his. "Actually, it's a good idea. I like the sound of it."

"What?" Rose shot her a lethal stare. "The ranch was named long before the Conrads bought it," she pointed out.

Trisha shrugged. "It's just a name."

Josh blinked. Talk about a killer look. Why did Rose and Trisha snap at each other?

"Actually, it's named after the Hohokam Indian tribe," Simon went on. "They lived in this area years ago."

Mickey leaned forward. "Are there any Hohokams living here now?"

"Maybe their descendants," Roberto said. "But the Hohokams are gone."

"The tribe disappeared around five hundred

years ago," Simon explained. "Hohokam means 'The Vanished Ones.'"

"Vanished? Like . . . from a plague? Or a war?" Deirdre asked.

Gary snickered. "I think I saw this on *The X-Files*. A spaceship came and picked them up!"

"No one knows for sure what happened to them." Simon stacked empty platters and started back to the main kitchen. "It's a total mystery."

"That's one of the things we're hoping to learn from our excavation," Roberto said. He nodded toward the west end of the property. "We've already uncovered some Hohokam artifacts. Some pottery and tools. But I'm dying for a big find. A petroglyph would be great."

"Petro-*what*?" Trisha nudged him. "Translation?"

"That's a carving on rock," Josh said. "Sometimes a picture. Sometimes words."

Roberto stared at him, surprised. "So you're into this stuff?"

Josh shrugged. "Yeah, but I've never worked on a dig. I wouldn't mind a tour of your site."

"Yeah. Digging up sand under the hot sun," Gary murmured sarcastically. "Awesome."

"More like a treasure hunt," Deirdre said. "Count me in."

"Well . . . I don't know—" Roberto hesitated.

"It's a bad idea," Rose said.

"Come on." Trisha beamed Roberto a smile. "You always promised to show me around."

Gazing at her, Roberto softened. "You guys

71

have to promise to be careful. We can't disturb anything."

"Whatever you say," Josh said enthusiastically. This was great. An unexpected bonus. "So when is the best time to see the site?"

"No!" Rose cried suddenly, leaping up from the bench.

Josh felt his throat go dry as he saw the horror in her deep green eyes.

"No!" She stared from one face to another. Desperate. Pleading. "Please . . . promise me that you won't go there!"

Chapter Fourteen

An Indian Spirit?

Silence.

Everyone gaped at Rose.

"You can't disturb the site." She turned to Josh, and squeezed his hand. "Don't go, Josh. Please! I can't let anything happen to any of you."

"What's the big deal?" Josh asked.

Rose turned to Roberto. "Go on. Tell them."

Roberto's dark brows arched. "About the legend?" he scoffed. "No, thanks. I'll stick with reality."

"What part isn't real for you?" she snapped. "The two sick students?"

"Try food poisoning," he said.

"And the fire in the tent?"

He shrugged. "It was hit by lightning. We're lucky no one got hurt that day."

"Luck has nothing to do with it," Rose insisted.

"What are you guys talking about?" Josh asked.

Firelight glimmered in Rose's eyes. "Ever since they started digging on Hohokam Ranch, terrible things have been happening."

"Every dig has its share of accidents," Roberto said.

"Not accidents," Rose insisted. "La Amadora. She's protecting the site. She roams the ancient settlements in these mountains, protecting them from strangers."

"So what is she, a ghost?" Mickey asked.

"She was a respected elder in the Hohokam tribe," Rose said quietly. "A woman who held many powers. When she was alive, she enchanted creatures of the desert. Sometimes she still appears through animals. A snake may not be a snake at all. It may be La Amadora, rising up to strike."

Deirdre squirmed. "We *do* have screens on our windows, right?"

"So she's an Indian spirit?" Josh asked Rose.

"She's the great protector. Sometimes she appears as a wild animal. Other times people see her in a red hooded cape. She creeps over the buried villages."

As if in a trance, Rose held her arms out and swayed. "Guarding. Searching for the force that made her tribe disappear. Howling an angry cry. A cry of revenge."

A high-pitched moan cut through the dark night.

Josh turned away from Rose.

It was Roberto, howling like a coyote. He yelped again, then laughed.

Rose spun around to glare at him. "You think you're funny?"

Roberto shrugged. "Give us a break, Rose. It's just a legend, a myth."

"Oh, really?" Her voice wavered with emotion. "Then what about Ben?"

"Ben Granger?" Trisha's eyes narrowed.

"What happened to him?" Josh asked.

Roberto stared down at the ground. "He was found in a ditch. Dead. His neck was broken."

"A ditch?" Rose shook her head. "A ditch that was dug by the archaeologists. He got too close. Too close to the Hohokam."

"That's not what I heard," Trisha insisted. "Ben lost his footing and fell. It was an accident. Right?" She gazed at the faces around the fire.

"Right?" she repeated.

Josh poured himself one last cup of hot chocolate as a spark flew out of the dying fire. It was late, and people were heading back to their rooms.

Slinging on his jacket, Mickey leaned close to Josh. "I'll catch you back at the room."

Josh frowned. "What's up?"

"Deirdre is creeped out about the ghost lady. I'm going to make sure she gets back to her room." Mickey grinned. "At least, I'll get her back before sunrise."

"Whoa. Mickey . . ." Josh shook his head.

"Thought you were going with Dana."

"Dana isn't here. Deirdre is the next best thing." Mickey zipped his jacket and raked his hair off his forehead. "Don't wait up."

Mickey headed off, hurrying up beside Deirdre. Roberto had left earlier. Gary and Trisha had already disappeared. Where was Rose?

Gone.

Josh wanted a few minutes alone with Rose, a chance to talk. Really talk. But she had already disappeared. As usual, his timing was off.

He stretched out on the wooden table and stared up at the wide black sky. Thousands of stars. You never saw this many stars back in Shadyside.

Shadyside . . . He thought about his sister Josie. He spoke to her on the phone before dinner. She sounded so bored, so depressed.

Josie has got to get out more, he decided. She's always home complaining about how boring her life is. But it's partly her own fault.

His thoughts moved to Rose. So what was the deal with her?

She'd spent a lot of time with him that day. Shopping. Driving. Talking.

And he liked hanging around with her. Definitely.

Did she feel the same way?

She seemed to hold herself back. She seemed to have something on her mind. . . .

A sharp noise cut through Josh's thoughts.

76

He bolted up.

A high wail echoed across the dark ranch.

A cry. A *human* cry?

An eerie, desperate cry that made Josh's hair stand on end.

Chapter Fifteen

Into the Pit

Josh slid down from the table and spun around.

Who was wailing like that? *Was* it a person? Or an animal?

He peered into the darkness. But he saw . . . nothing.

The wail shattered the night again. Hollow.

A cry of pain.

A woman's cry?

Rose's story filled his mind. The woman wearing a red cape. Floating over the ruins. Wailing. Crying out for revenge.

Okay, the cry *sounded* like a woman. But Josh knew that lots of desert animals made strange sounds. Especially at night, under the cover of darkness.

And if it was a desert animal—maybe he'd be smart to get inside.

78

The eerie wail repeated as Josh crossed the green meadow. Passing the barn and the fenced-in corral, he wished that someone else was with him. Mickey would joke about it. Trisha might be able to identify the animal.

Another shrieking wail—and Josh broke into a run. His feet pounded the dirt as he followed the path back to the main buildings.

At last—the west lobby.

Josh flipped open the screen door—

And nearly crashed into Roberto.

"Whoa!" Roberto stepped back. "Take it easy, man."

"That noise," Josh said, his chest heaving painfully. "Did you hear it? A high wail."

Roberto's dark eyes narrowed. "La Amadora?"

"Or an animal," Josh said. "I don't know. Listen."

Silence.

Roberto shrugged. "Nothing. It could be a coyote." He grinned. "Either that or Casper the Friendly Ghost."

Josh glared at him. "Wait. I'm not making this up—"

"See you tomorrow," Roberto said, stepping through the screen door.

"So what do you think it was?" Mickey asked when Josh told him about the wailing sound. "A desert bird? Or a wolf or something?"

Josh sat up on his bed, his chin tucked against the knees of his sweatpants. It was late, but he couldn't sleep. "I don't think wolves live around here," Josh replied. "Coyotes probably do. But it didn't sound like an animal. I'd swear it was a person."

"Someone could have been hiding behind the barn. Fooling around. Trisha. Or Rose." Mickey tossed his hair back. "Face it. That Rose is a little weird." He waved his hands and mimicked: "La Amadora! La Amadora!"

Josh sighed. "Ha, ha. You're funny. Remind me to laugh later."

"Whatever." Mickey leaned against the windowsill. "All I know is, Roberto is being a total jerk about the dig. Like we're going to barrel through there and ruin the ruins."

"Yeah, and he's a big-shot archaeologist. Even though he's—what?—a year older than us?"

Mickey nodded. "And if Rose has any say, we'll *never* get to see it."

Josh really wanted to see it. He was so close to an actual dig. No way could he go home without checking it out.

"Do you think we could find it? Like . . . *now?*" Josh asked.

Mickey grinned. "Now is good."

That's the great thing about Mickey, Josh decided as they grabbed flashlights and jackets and headed out into the cool desert night. Mickey can change plans. Instantly. And he's up for anything. Especially if it makes no sense!

"So," Josh said. "Any idea where this thing is?"

Mickey shrugged. "When we were swimming, I saw a bunch of workers going back and forth on the path."

"They said the other end of the ranch," Josh recalled. "Could be far away."

"Well, they were all walking," Mickey said. "So it can't be that far."

"Good. The thought of you saddling up a horse scares me," Josh joked.

"Scares *you*?!" Mickey laughed. "Think about the poor horse."

The buildings of the west wing disappeared in the darkness as they approached the pools. Underwater lights glowed beneath the still waters. Tempting. But Josh had his mind set.

He was going to see the dig.

"You realize what we're doing is totally insane. What time is it?" Josh asked as they turned onto the path near the gazebos.

Mickey shrugged. "Ten? Twelve? Two? Doesn't matter. It's spring break, man. It's the time to do insane things—right?"

Circles of white from their flashlights bounced eerily along the path.

A shrill voice cut through the air.

The guys froze.

"Did you hear that?" Mickey asked.

"I'm not deaf." Josh felt his pulse racing. Not again. Please.

"Waaaaaaaaay!"

Mickey glanced back, as if he was too afraid to move. "Is it her? That Indian ghost?"

"La Amadora?" Josh whispered, trying to

keep his legs from trembling.

Josh didn't believe in ghosts. He didn't even buy into all the stuff about the Senior Class Curse.

So why was he petrified now?

"Waaaaait!" the voice cried. *"Mickey."*

Hold on, Josh thought. That's not the voice I heard before.

"Mickey!"

They turned around to see someone running up the path behind them.

Deirdre.

"Forget what I said about that ghost stuff," Mickey told Josh. "I was just trying to scare you."

By the time Deirdre caught up to them, she was out of breath. "What does it take to get your attention?" she gasped.

Josh grinned. "You did a pretty good job."

Deirdre held a hand to her chest and took a deep breath. "I saw you guys leave the west wing. Then it hit me. Trisha's out with Gary. That left me completely alone. The only one in the whole building. Kind of scary."

Mickey linked his arm through hers. "Don't worry. We'll protect you."

She grinned at him. "I knew I could count on you."

Mickey and Deirdre? Josh thought. Wow. I don't believe how she's looking at him. Has she forgotten that he's her sister's boyfriend?

Typical Mickey, Josh thought with more than a little envy. He's such a total goof. Why do girls think he's so terrific?

"So . . . what are you guys doing out here, anyway?" Deirdre asked as they walked along the path, toward the inky-black mountains.

"We're going to check out the dig," Mickey said. "Josh wants to meet the ghost."

"You're kidding." Deirdre stared back at Josh. "Right? Kidding?"

"Nope," Josh said. "We really are going to the dig."

"You guys are crazy. And I'm nuts to go along with you." Deirdre pressed her face into Mickey's shoulder. "Just let me know when the scary part is over."

Josh rolled his eyes.

Continuing down the path, passing dark, sloping hills, they walked steadily for at least fifteen minutes. Finally Josh saw it.

Squares of desert were roped off and marked with flags. Sort of a grid. In parts the ground was dug up. Other areas were still untouched sand and clay, dotted by weeds. Scraggly bushes. Cacti. Spiny aloe plants.

"This must be it." Josh ran ahead to the site.

This was where they would do the digging. Uncovering things from hundreds of years ago.

What if he found something on his own?

Awesome!

"This place is kinda creepy," Deirdre complained. "Especially at night."

"Sort of like a graveyard," Mickey chimed in. "Without the headstones. I wish we knew a Hohokam chant. Something to wake up the dead."

83

"Don't even say that," Deirdre snapped. "The whole tribe disappeared! What if their spirits *are* still out here—waiting for their revenge?"

Josh squatted beside a shallow trench. The clay was chiseled away, revealing a darker layer of soil.

Did the archaeologists think something was buried there?

He brushed at the dirt.

"Listen!" Deirdre froze. "What was that?"

Josh stopped digging and waited.

Scraping noises . . . far away. The sound of something moving in the sand.

"What *is* that?" Deirdre cried.

"It's definitely a ghost," Mickey teased. "Or a spirit rising up from the dead." He laughed. He enjoyed making Deirdre shiver.

Josh rolled his eyes. "The desert is full of lizards and jackrabbits and snakes."

"Snakes?" Deirdre grabbed Mickey's arm. "Like that's going to make me feel better? Let's go."

"Hold on," Josh insisted. "Just give me a minute to check this place out. We came all the way here."

"Don't worry," Mickey told Deirdre. "I'll protect you. Just stay close. Very close," he added, wrapping her in his arms.

Josh turned away as they started kissing. Mickey is unbelievable, he thought.

Josh paused to survey a group of dark pits.

That's probably where they found the

Hohokam tools, he thought. He headed toward them.

He stopped about a foot away from a hole. He didn't want to get too close, in case the sides collapsed.

His flashlight swept over the pit. It was wide and deep—about five feet. And neatly carved. It had to be slow, painstaking work.

Josh turned away and heard a scuffling noise behind him. Another lizard?

Something pressed into his back.

Definitely not a lizard. Something bigger.

Fear rippled down his spine. "Hey, what's—?"

It pushed him. Hard.

Josh lost his balance.

He pitched forward, arms flailing at the air.

And then he was falling . . .

Falling . . .

Into the bottomless darkness.

Chapter Sixteen

Don't Go There!

Josh hit solid ground with a grunt.

How far had he fallen?

Just a few feet. Into in a wide ditch— a dried riverbed at the edge of the excavation.

Stunned, heart pounding, he raised his head.

Who pushed me? he wondered. Who—or *what*?

He struggled to focus. Darkness everywhere. No one in sight. And then he saw two dancing flashlight beams. Mickey and Deirdre came into view, jumping over a roped-off area.

"Josh!" Deirdre called. "Are you okay? What are you doing down there?"

Standing up, Josh brushed off his hands and knees. "Did you see who it was?" he asked breathlessly. "Who pushed me?"

"Huh? Pushed you?" Mickey cried.

"I . . . I didn't see anyone," Deirdre said, glancing around nervously. "Are you sure you were pushed?"

"Yeah. Very sure," Josh murmured.

Deirdre tugged her hair back, so hard she seemed ready to pull it out. "Let's go. Please," she begged. "Josh—climb out of there."

Josh took a deep breath. He still felt shaky. Stepping to the edge of the ditch, he heard a crunch under his sneaker.

What was that?

Squatting, he aimed his flashlight—and saw yellowed fragments. Pieces of something. Bones?

Pottery. He must have crushed it when he stepped on it.

Carefully he gathered the pieces.

Mickey reached out a hand to pull him out. Josh decided to keep quiet. He tucked the pieces into a pocket of his jacket and climbed out of the ditch.

I'll have to show it to Roberto, he decided. I hope it isn't important. I hope he isn't angry that I crunched it.

"You moron!" Roberto growled the next morning. "I told you to stay away from the site unless I guided you!"

"I'm really sorry," Josh said, staring at the broken shards of pottery. He hadn't eaten much breakfast. He was nervous about showing the pottery to Roberto.

"I hoped it wasn't important," Josh said. "I

didn't find this on the site. It was in a ditch. A few feet from the roped-off area."

"As if that matters." Roberto frowned as he turned the fragments over in his hand.

"Do you think it's from the Hohokam tribe?" Josh asked hopefully. "I mean, is it a good find?"

"Now that it's crushed? Not really." Roberto dropped the pieces into a small cloth sack. "I'll show the archaeologists. They'll probably want to excavate the ditch where you found this."

Josh nodded. "Great."

Disapproval gleamed in Roberto's dark eyes. "From now on, stay away from the excavation."

"Right. Except today," Josh pointed out. "You promised to show us the site."

Roberto glared and headed back into the building. He slammed the screen door behind him.

So he's annoyed, Josh thought. He'll get over it.

Eventually.

Later that morning they hiked to the site. Josh still felt guilty, but everyone else was in a good mood. In the daylight Josh saw that the trail was lined by colorful wildflowers.

"We had a wet winter," Rose explained. "Now everything is growing like crazy."

Roberto was cool to Josh. So cool that Gary noticed.

"What's the deal with him?" Gary asked as he fell into step beside Josh. "He's had you carrying the pack since we left the ranch."

Josh strained under the weight as he forged ahead. Roberto had loaded a backpack with canteens and a first-aid kit. All the necessities.

But did Josh have to tow the weight—all the way there?

Not that Mickey cared. He looked cool and casual, adjusting his baseball cap against the sun. Rose walked along dreamily, lost in thought. And Deirdre and Trisha were too busy gathering wildflowers to notice anyone else.

"I messed up last night," Josh confessed. "I guess Roberto is the kind of guy who holds a grudge."

Gary gritted his teeth as he stared at their guide. "I can hold a grudge, too. He's starting to steam me."

"Take it easy," Josh warned. He knew that Gary was annoyed because Trisha had been flirting with Roberto.

He turned to see Roberto tuck a fat lavender wildflower behind Trisha's ear.

"Look at him," Gary muttered. "Making a move on Trisha, right in front of me. Does he think I'm blind?"

"Do me a favor," Josh said. "If you're planning to pound the guy, could you wait until after he shows us the site? I'd sort of like the complete tour."

Gary just frowned and pressed up the hill. He moved quickly to catch up with Trisha.

Trudging behind him, Josh climbed steadily until the excavation site came into view.

Josh frowned. He had expected to see archaeologists kneeling in the roped-off grid. But the site was empty.

"Where is everyone?" Josh asked.

"It's Saturday," Roberto pointed out. "The crew has the day off. But I'll explain the layout of the site."

He led them up to the first pit, then held up his hands. "Just stay on the trail. The site can be dangerous for you. And I'll be in big trouble if somebody interferes with the dig," Roberto said, glaring at Josh.

"We started digging here because of Hohokam legend," Roberto began. He explained how a drawing on a rock had named this location as sacred ground.

Josh lowered the backpack and wiped his sweaty hands.

Roberto pointed out the pit where they'd found the tools. He explained how the workers preserved the items they uncovered. He showed them the flags that marked the location of their finds. Then he led the group along the trail that circled the site.

Josh nearly plowed into Rose when she stopped short in front of him.

"No, wait!" Rose squeezed her eyes shut and shook her head. "We're too close to the ruins. The Hohokam will be disturbed!"

"Give me a break, Rose," Trisha said. "Besides, the site is on my property. And we're not going to hurt anything."

"No!" Rose shouted. "You're getting too

close!" Her long, dark hair flew as she shook her head furiously. "La Amadora is near. I can feel it!"

Trisha spun around, hands on her hips. "Will you stop with this La Amadora stuff? Nothing is going to happen to us!"

"You're wrong!" Rose insisted. "*Please!*"

Trisha rolled her eyes. She turned and continued up the narrow trail. She joined Roberto at the front of the group, climbing the ridge.

Hoisting the backpack, Josh moved ahead.

"No!" Rose pushed her hands against his chest, trying to stop him.

He paused, glancing at the rest of the group.

He watched Trisha forge ahead. She scuttled to the top of the ridge.

He watched her straighten up, outlined by the cloudless blue sky. She shielded her eyes with one hand and gazed around.

Then Trisha opened her mouth in a scream of horror.

"What's wrong?" Josh cried.

Trisha's body trembled wildly. Then she collapsed to the ground and didn't move.

Chapter Seventeen

Trisha's Horror

Josh dropped the backpack and raced up the trail. Mickey and Deirdre were close behind him.

"Trisha!" Deirdre kneeled beside her. "What's wrong? What is it?"

Trisha slowly opened her eyes. She gasped for breath. She stared up at them blankly, as if she didn't recognize them.

Did she faint? Josh wondered. Or was it something she saw up here?

"Give her some air!" Roberto ordered. "Get back!"

"Why don't *you* back off?" Gary snapped, pushing Roberto away from Trisha. "This whole hike was a stupid idea. *Your* stupid idea."

"What's your problem?" Roberto snapped. "Nobody was forced to come along."

Gary turned away and took Trisha's hand. "You're okay? Are you? Tell us what's wrong."

Trisha squeezed her eyes shut and shook her head.

When she finally opened her eyes, the familiar spark had returned. She took a deep breath and whispered, "I—I had a vision. It was horrible."

She's okay, Josh thought with relief. Just another one of her psychic flashes.

"Come down from there!" Rose called to the group. She hadn't moved from the bottom of the ridge. "Please! We have to leave the ruins—before something else happens."

"Hold your horses," Gary called down impatiently. "Someone fainted up here—or didn't you notice?"

"I just got this flash," Trisha said, hugging her sides. "It was overwhelming."

Roberto seemed confused. "What's going on?"

Josh stepped back. He was concerned about Trisha. But he didn't buy all the stuff about her predictions. She believed she could see the future.

Last spring Trisha had a vision that the senior class was cursed. That the seniors would die before graduation.

Some kids started calling it the Doom Class.

Josh didn't believe Trisha's predictions.

Yes, some tragic things had happened at Shadyside High this year. But it was bad luck, Josh decided. Just bad luck.

He glanced up at Mickey, who rolled his

eyes. Mickey didn't buy the package, either.

Rose edged closer to the group, frightened but curious.

"You're okay now," Gary said, hugging Trisha. "You're going to be fine."

"But what was it about?" Deirdre asked. "What did you see?"

"At first I saw a coyote," Trisha answered. "A coyote—with red stripes. Strange, huh?"

"There are coyotes in this desert," Roberto pointed out. "Sometimes they're a problem. Usually they avoid the populated areas."

"Did it attack?" Deirdre asked. "Did somebody get hurt?"

"It's not clear." Trisha's brown eyes clouded with confusion. "The coyote was angry. Howling."

"Not a good sign," Mickey said, snickering.

"And when it cried out, that's when I realized we were there—all of us." Her eyes skimmed the group. "Gary and I. Deirdre. Josh and Mickey."

Deirdre dropped onto her knees beside Trisha. "What does it mean?"

"I don't know." Trisha shook her head. "But as the coyote howled, we all scattered."

"Why?" Deirdre insisted. "Where did we go?"

Trisha closed her eyes to concentrate. "We flew through the air. Then we vanished."

"Vanished . . . just like the Hohokam tribe," Deirdre said softly. She shuddered. "Okay, this is scary. Really scary."

"Whoa, wait," Mickey said, pulling Deirdre to

her feet. "Don't freak. It's not going to come true. We don't even know what it means!"

"But, what *does* it mean?" Deirdre asked, gazing from one friend to another.

"Look, it's hot. We've been hiking the entire morning. The altitude here is probably different than at your home," Roberto said calmly. "There are a zillion explanations."

"No."

Everyone turned to Rose. Her green eyes flashed excitedly. "It's La Amadora. She caused the vision. She is coming."

Rose turned back to the site at the bottom of the ridge. A dry wind rippled the flags on the ruins.

"La Amadora is coming," Rose said. "She will make something terrible happen."

"Great," Mickey muttered under his breath. "Now we have *two* psychic friends. What is this—a contest?"

"Let's blow this graveyard," Gary suggested. "I say we go back and hang by the pool."

"Okay, fine," Roberto replied, eyeing him coldly. "We can go back—if you're scared."

Gary's face reddened. "Whoa. I'm not scared. It's just that—"

"Let's hike down to the saguaro cactus forest," Roberto suggested. "Some of the cacti there are over a hundred years old. One of them is forty feet tall."

"But Trisha isn't feeling well," Gary argued. "And who cares about some—"

"I'm okay," Trisha interrupted, leaning on

Gary's arm. "And the cactus forest—it's so awesome. Really. You'll like it."

"Just as long as we get away from the ruins," Rose insisted, clenching her eyes shut. "La Amadora . . . she's been disturbed. We need to leave here."

Everyone filed down the trail leaving Josh alone with the backpack. With a groan, he hoisted it onto his shoulders.

Next time we stop, Josh thought, I'm tossing this thing over to Mickey.

The sun beat down on them. It was almost like walking in an oven.

Josh was relieved when the trail finally cut into the cactus forest. At least the tall and imposing saguaro cacti with uplifted arms provided some shade from the blistering sunlight.

Deirdre stared up at a cactus that towered over her. "So where are the cactus flowers?"

"They bloom at night," Rose explained. "And in the summer the blossoms ripen into fruit. Some local tribes, like the Hohokam, used to eat the fruit like candy. They also boiled it down for jam or syrup."

"Right," Roberto agreed. "My family is descended from the Yaqui tribe. My ancestors used the fruit of the saguaro cactus for ceremonial wine."

"Yeah," Mickey joked, "but it's a drag when the thorns get stuck between your teeth!"

"I hate when that happens!" Gary sneered.

Roberto glared at them but didn't say anything.

"I need a break," Trisha said. "Where's the water?"

"In the pack." Roberto slid the backpack off Josh's shoulders and pulled out two canteens. "Here we go."

"I need a break, too," Josh told Roberto. "How about getting someone else to carry this pack?"

"You're lucky I even let you come along." Roberto glared at Josh. "After what you did . . . you should be hauling boulders for the next twenty years."

"Whoa," Trisha said, taking the canteens from Roberto's hands and backing away. "A little tension here?"

"Give me a break," Josh told Roberto. "I didn't mean to break the pottery. At least I found something, right?"

Roberto shook his head. "Don't kid yourself, Josh. You're not part of the dig."

"I'm sorry, okay?" Josh said.

"No, Josh. It's not okay. You were reckless, and I'm not going to forget it."

Josh stared as Roberto turned away. Talk about *cold*! He wasn't going to be hanging out with Roberto anytime soon.

Trisha filled a few cups and handed them out. Josh took his cup over to a boulder and slumped down. The hike was a total failure. Maybe it was the heat. Maybe it was Trisha's vision . . . or Roberto's grudge . . . or the way Rose freaked out about La Amadora.

Josh noticed ruts in the sand. Animal burrows.

Roberto had said that the Sonoran Desert was loaded with animals. Some of them came out only at night.

"Hey, Josh." Trisha sat down on the rock beside him.

"Feeling better?" he asked.

She shrugged. "I just wish I knew what that vision meant. I mean, what if it *was* some kind of warning?"

"Right," Josh said, staring at the ground. "Like, beware of coyotes with red stripes."

He heard a soft buzzing sound. It stopped after a few seconds. Josh ignored it.

"Don't make fun," she scolded. She turned away from him.

The buzzing started again. What was that?

Josh turned—and saw a snake slither out of the burrow.

It wasn't a buzz. It was a rattle.

A rattlesnake!

"Look out!" Josh yelled. He sprang off the rock.

Trisha gasped.

Before she could move, the snake snapped its head forward—and sank its fangs into her leg.

Chapter Eighteen

La Amadora Strikes?

"**J**osh!" Trisha's eyes were pleading, desperate as she collapsed onto the ground. Leaning over her, Josh saw the red marks on her calf.

Two deep punctures about an inch apart.

"She's been bitten!" Josh shouted to the others. "I saw it! It was a rattlesnake!"

The snake scuttled between the rocks, disappearing quickly.

"Trisha!" Josh's knees hit the dirt as he leaned over her. He squeezed her hand.

"Are you okay?" he demanded. "Can you hear me?"

She didn't squeeze back. Her hand was limp. Lifeless.

"Where is the bite?" Roberto called.

"On her leg," Josh told him. "Her calf. Just below her shorts."

Everyone clustered around.

"Is she going to be all right?" Gary asked, picking up Trisha's hand. "She—she's unconscious!"

"Probably from shock," Roberto answered. "And fright. Rose, get your father on the radio. Tell him to bring the jeep to the entrance of Saguaro Forest. Everyone else, step back. Now!"

Everyone followed Roberto's orders. Even Gary. Rose took a two-way radio out of the backpack. "Rose to Hohokam Ranch. Dad, are you there?"

Josh heard static crackle as Rose moved away from the group to send the message.

"Okay," Roberto said. "We need to elevate the rest of her body." He pointed to Gary and Josh. "Lift her onto the boulder at my count. One, two, three . . ."

Together they picked Trisha up and positioned her onto Gary's lap. Roberto tied a constriction band on her leg, a few inches above the bite. Then he poured water over the bite marks.

"What about a serum?" Mickey asked. "Isn't there a serum for snakebites?"

Gary nodded. "In the movies they *suck* out the venom."

"I've got the serum in the kit. But we're less than thirty minutes from the hospital," Roberto said calmly. "She's better off getting treated there."

"Dad was working close by," Rose called to

them. "He'll be here in five minutes."

"This is so awful." Deirdre reached down and pushed a strand of Trisha's hair out of her eyes.

"I'm sorry . . . sorry I've been trying to scare everyone," Rose stammered. "It's just that . . ." Her voice trailed off.

"We don't blame you for what happened to Trisha," Josh told her.

"You see how bad things happen out here," Rose said, her voice trembling. "I hope it isn't La Amadora. I hope it was just a rattlesnake. . . ."

Everyone stared at her.

"Please don't blame me," Rose continued, lowering her eyes to Trisha's still body. "I was only trying to help. I thought if I warned you . . ."

The hum of an engine interrupted her. The jeep appeared, blazing down the narrow trail.

"Trisha is going to be okay," Roberto said as Simon slammed on the brakes and jumped out. "Just go back to the ranch."

Josh watched as Roberto and Simon lifted Trisha into the back of the jeep.

Was she going to be okay?

Were they *all* going to be okay?

Rose was so frightened, so certain that this tribal spirit was real.

Did Rose know something they didn't?

PART FOUR

Chapter Nineteen

Wanna Play—Again?

J osie laughed. She tossed a napkin across
the table to Tim. "Look at your face!" she
cried. "It's bright orange!"

Tim grabbed the napkin and wiped the
spaghetti sauce from his cheeks and chin.

"I can't take him anywhere," Evan said,
shaking his head.

"Spaghetti is too hard to eat," Tim protested.
"I'm better with finger foods. You know. Like
this meatball." He lifted the meatball off his
plate with one hand and took a big bite of it.

"Gross," Jennifer declared, laughing. "That's
totally gross."

"That's something Matty Winger would do!"
Josie declared.

Tim looked hurt. "Who's Matty Winger? Is he
a great guy, too?"

"No. He's a total geek."

They all laughed.

Evan demonstrated for Tim the proper way to eat spaghetti. He used a fork and a tablespoon and rolled the spaghetti against the spoon. "See? Perfect?"

It was perfect—until Tim slapped the spoon—and the rolled-up spaghetti went flying into Evan's lap.

More wild laughter. Josie laughed so hard she started to choke.

She saw people staring at them across the crowded restaurant. A waitress was shaking her head.

We're making a nuisance of ourselves, she realized. But I don't care. I'm having such a great time!

I can't believe I didn't like these guys last night, Josie thought. Why are my first impressions of people always wrong?

She smiled across the checkered tablecloth at Tim. She realized she liked him a *lot*. He was so funny. And he seemed really smart and quick. His eyes were always flashing, dancing around, as if hiding some kind of funny secret.

I wonder if he likes me, too? Josie thought.

The guys had called during the afternoon. Then that night they picked Jennifer and Josie up in the blue van and drove to the Spaghetti House, an enormous family restaurant on the other side of Waynesbridge.

Josie and Jennifer both had their doubts about seeing the guys again. "But we need an adventure," Jennifer insisted. "We need a spring break adventure."

Josie hoped it wasn't *too much* of an adventure. The scrawled words on Jennifer's windshield lingered all day in her mind: WANNA PLAY?

Were Evan and Tim responsible? Of course not. It didn't seem possible.

But then—who?

The evil spirit? The evil spirit she had unleashed in Jennifer's house when she uttered the ancient words of the Doom Spell?

No. Please—no!

Josie had never told Jennifer about the spell. About the evil that threatened to doom everyone in the senior class. Josie had kept the secret from everyone.

She prayed that the spirit was gone. That it wasn't responsible for the frightening, tragic events that haunted her year as a senior. She prayed that the spirit wasn't out there somewhere, waiting to finish its evil mission, to murder everyone in the class.

Last night, when she saw the words in red paint—WANNA PLAY?—she thought of the evil spirit first.

But that was crazy. *Crazy!*

Some idiot from the bar had painted those words. Someone she didn't even know.

That's what Josie wanted to believe. That's what she forced herself to believe.

She didn't want to think about it at all. She wanted to relax and have fun with these new guys. She wanted to get to know Tim better. . . .

She wanted to laugh.

He was making her laugh. Trying to juggle two meatballs in the air. Josie laughed so hard, Coke went up her nose. She choked again.

She jumped up. Excused herself. Hurried into the brightly lit rest room.

She glanced down the row of sinks. Saw a high, open window at the end of a row of stalls. No one else in here.

Josie turned on a cold water faucet. Leaned over the sink. Splashed water on her face.

She dried herself off with a paper towel, then studied her face in the mirror. She pulled the hairbrush from her bag and had just started to brush her hair—when she heard the harsh whisper.

"Wanna play?"

"Huh?" Startled, she dropped the hairbrush into the sink.

She grabbed it up, then spun around. "Who's here?"

"Wanna play?" the rasping whisper said again.

Coming from the closed stall at the end of the row?

"Is someone in here?" Josie called, her voice higher, tighter than she expected. "Hey—who is it?"

"Wanna play?"

Josie peered beneath the stall. No feet. No one in there.

Her heart pounding, she edged into the stall next to it. Stood on the toilet. Pulled herself up

108

so that she could see over the top.

No. Empty. No one in the stall.

"Wanna play?"

The voice so hoarse, so cold, so chilling.

"Who are you?" Josie cried. "Where are you?"

A sob escaped her throat. "What do you want? Why are you *doing* this?"

Chapter Twenty

An Adventure

Josie hurried back to the table. I'm not going to say anything, she decided. I'm not going to tell Jennifer what happened. I don't want to spoil this evening.

"Hey—where's Evan?" she asked.

"Went to the men's room," Tim replied. "Didn't you pass him on the way?"

Josie dropped into her seat.

"Are you okay?" Jennifer asked. "You look so pale."

"It's just these lights," Josie replied. "I'm fine."

Thank goodness you can't see my legs trembling, she thought.

Is someone *stalking* me? Is it the evil spirit?

Is Jennifer being stalked, too?

She glanced at Evan's empty chair. Could it have been Evan? Whispering from outside the rest room window?

He appeared a few seconds later. Picked up his white cloth napkin. Snapped it at Tim.

"Evan, did you go outside?" Josie asked.

"Huh?" He squinted at her. "Outside? No. I went to the john. Why? What's outside?" he asked innocently.

Josie could feel her face growing hot. She knew she was blushing.

"Let's get out of this place," Tim suggested, wiping more spaghetti sauce off his chin. "We'll ride around or something."

"Hey—let's go up to River Ridge!" Jennifer suggested. "It's such a perfect spring night. It'll be beautiful up there!"

River Ridge? Josie glared at Jennifer. Was she out of her mind? River Ridge, a high cliff overlooking the Conononka River, was the most popular makeout spot in town for Shadyside High kids.

Wow. Jennifer must really have the hots for Evan, Josie decided.

Am I ready to go up there with Tim? she asked herself.

Don't think about it. Just do it. It's an adventure, remember?

Josie peered out the window as the van climbed, following the curving River Road up to the black rock cliffs overlooking Shadyside. The pale half-moon appeared to be winking down at her. Stars glittered in the purple night sky.

Tim had cranked the radio way up. An old Rolling Stones song shook the car.

Josie turned and studied Tim. His eyes caught the moonlight as he gazed through the windshield. He's really cute, Josie thought. He had one hand on the wheel, the other on the back of her seat.

The road flattened out as they reached the top of the cliff. Tim drove past several cars parked along the grassy area that led to the cliff. The van bumped over rocks on the road. Tim pulled to a stop at a deserted area where the road ended.

He cut off the lights and the engine. Then he turned to Josie with a smile. "Nice night," he said.

"How about a walk?" Evan suggested from behind them. He pushed open his door and jumped out. Then he took Jennifer's hands and tugged her out.

"Wow! You can see the whole town down there!" Jennifer exclaimed, gazing over the cliff edge.

Evan laughed. "You mean you've never been up here before?"

Even in the pale moonlight Josie could see Jennifer blush. "Maybe. Maybe not," she said coyly.

Tim walked across the tall grass to the cliff edge. "What's at the bottom?" He peered down. "Jagged black rocks. Then the river."

"The mighty Conononka!" Josie declared. "You can smell it all the way up here." She inhaled deeply. "Smells good, actually. So fresh."

She turned to see Evan slide his arm around Jennifer's shoulders. Jennifer shivered and leaned against him. A gust of wind blew her hair against Evan's face.

Jennifer and Evan walked off, leaning against each other. Josie watched them cross the grass toward the trees on the other side of the road.

"Josie, come over here," Tim called. He motioned to her. He hadn't moved from the cliff edge. "The view is amazing!"

Josie hesitated. "I—I'm a little afraid of heights," she stammered.

"You've *got* to see this," he insisted. "Come here. You'll be okay. I'll hold on to you."

Hold on to me? I kind of *like* that idea, Josie thought.

She made her way carefully across the grass to the rocky cliff edge. Tim took her hand. Then he stepped behind her and put his hands on her shoulders.

"I've got you," he said softly. "Look down."

Josie gazed down at the sharp, jagged rocks below, splashed by the flowing river water. The river sparkled, golden in the moonlight. Beyond the water the town of Shadyside stretched into the darkness, like a miniature toy town.

Tim held her firmly. "Where is your house?" he asked in just above a whisper. "Show me."

She could feel his warm breath on the back of her neck. It gave her a chill.

Josie pointed to the right. "Somewhere over

113

there, I think. See that church? The white steeple? My house is two blocks behind it."

"Nice way up here," Tim said softly. "You feel you can take off and fly."

"N-not really," Josie stammered.

He stood so close behind her. She felt his arms slide around her waist.

She thought he was going to kiss her.

But instead, his hands moved back up to her shoulders. And he whispered in her ear, "*Do you like scary movies?*"

"Huh?" Josie reacted with surprise. "What?"

"*Do you like scary movies?*" Tim repeated in a hoarse whisper.

And then he pushed her off the cliff.

Chapter Twenty-one

Wanna Play Rough?

Josie let out a shriek as she tumbled forward.

Her cry was cut off by Tim's strong hands circling her waist.

With a groan he tugged her back. They stumbled and fell together onto the grass.

"Are you okay?" Tim demanded breathlessly. "Josie—are you okay?" He still had his arms wrapped tightly around her.

"I—I guess," she managed to choke out. Her heart pounded against her chest. She had a shrill ringing in her ears.

"Oh, wow. I'm so sorry," Tim said, finally loosening his hold on her. He sat up beside her and helped pull her up. "I'm so sorry, Josie. Wow. That was so scary. What a close call!"

She saw that he was breathing hard, too. He

115

let out a long sigh of relief. "What a close call," he repeated, shaking his head.

The ringing in Josie's ears faded. "A close call?" she cried. "You—you *pushed* me—!"

"No!" Tim protested. "I slipped, Josie. I slipped on the wet grass. And . . . oh, thank goodness—I grabbed you in time."

"You . . . slipped?" Josie asked, locking her eyes on his. "But what was that question you asked me, Tim? Why did you ask me about scary movies?"

"I—I remembered a scary movie I saw a few weeks ago," he stammered. "It ended on a high cliff. Just like this one. The cliff reminded me, that's all. So I asked if you like scary movies."

He swallowed. "Then I slipped and . . . and . . ."

Is he telling the truth? Josie wondered.

Was it an accident? Did he save my life?

Before she could think about her questions, Tim's arms were around her. And he was kissing her, pressing his warm lips hard against hers. Kissing her . . . kissing her so *fiercely* . . .

Josie slept late the next morning. And woke up remembering Tim's kisses.

"He was so sweet," she murmured to herself.

A few minutes later she made her way down to the kitchen, still in her nightshirt, her hair tangled and unbrushed.

"You were out late last night," her mom greeted her.

"Yeah, I guess." Josie yawned.

"Josh called," Mrs. Maxwell reported, pouring herself a mug of coffee.

"How's he doing?" Josie asked, pulling a carton of orange juice from the refrigerator.

"Okay, I guess," her mother replied. "He was acting kind of mysterious. Like there was something going on he didn't want to tell me about. But you know Josh. He can't keep any kind of secret."

Josie nodded. She thought about Tim again, about how he held her so tightly, how he kissed her.

"Do me a favor," her mom said, interrupting her thoughts. "Bring in the newspaper. I forgot."

Josie set down the orange juice carton. Her bare feet slapped against the floor as she made her way to the front of the house.

She pulled open the door. Stepped out onto the front stoop.

And gasped as she read the words splashed in red paint across the walk:

WANNA PLAY ROUGH?

PART FIVE

Chapter Twenty-two

Lost in the Desert

A cool splash of water. Then total submersion.

Josh shot up to the surface and took a deep breath. The water felt great after a sweaty morning in the desert. Mickey swam by, doing laps, but no one else had showed at the pool.

"I stopped by Deirdre's room, but she wasn't into swimming," Mickey said.

"She's upset about Trisha," Josh explained.

Josh understood. He'd felt awful, seeing Trisha passed out like that. Carried into the jeep.

But Simon had called the ranch to pass the word that Trisha was fine. The doctors would release her tomorrow morning.

That night dinner was served in the west atrium. Rose helped the staff set out bowls of cheese, tomatoes, guacamole, and stewed meat for tacos.

As Josh filled taco shells at the buffet table, he heard Gary talking about his trip to the hospital that afternoon.

"Trisha looks great," Gary said. "Her leg is a little swollen, but it doesn't hurt."

Deirdre dropped her taco back onto her plate. "I still feel awful. What a nightmare."

"Hey, nobody died, right?" Mickey bit into a jalapeno and winced. "So how come this feels like a funeral?"

"Right." Gary pointed at Mickey. "And Trisha wants us to have fun. She said we should get into town tonight. There's a multiplex cinema at the mall. And there's a drive-in movie theater not far from here."

Mickey gave a thumbs-up. "I vote for the drive-in. Wow! I didn't know there were any drive-ins left!"

"You don't even know what's playing," Deirdre pointed out. "*Planet Warriors*," Rose said, calling across the atrium. "It's pretty good. I saw it last week."

"Sounds like a plan," Gary said.

Josh went over to the buffet table and started filling another taco. "Would you like to come along?" he asked Rose.

She shook her head. "I overdosed on space movies."

"Me, too," Josh lied. "I'll probably hang out here."

"Oh, really?" Rose seemed surprised and a

little tense. "Okay. So . . . if we're both going to be here, I guess, well—"

Josh studied her green eyes. So . . . she *was* nervous, too. He was glad that she felt the same way.

"What do you want to do?" he asked.

Rose stacked two platters. "I think we should find some place where we can talk, Josh. I want to know more about you." She grinned at him. "I want to know everything!"

"Everything?" Josh grinned back at her. Was she teasing him? Or was she serious? He couldn't tell.

"We've got all night," Rose said with a flash of green eyes.

Later, Josh pulled on a pair of jeans and combed his hair. He was falling for Rose, he realized. Rose Travis.

Rose . . . Rose . . . Her name repeated in his mind.

The ranch was dark and silent by the time she knocked on Josh's door. "Are the others still here?" she asked, peering into the room.

"They left. Half an hour ago."

"Good." Rose frowned. "Your friend Mickey? I don't think he likes me. Did I do something wrong?"

Josh shrugged. "Don't try to figure him out. I gave up years ago."

Rose's eyes sparkled as she smiled. "Grab a jacket. There's something I want you to see."

Pulling on his denim jacket, Josh followed

her out. "Where are we going?" he asked as she led him across the dark lawn.

"You'll see." She laughed, then raced ahead, past the barn.

Josh jogged after her. Rose had the best laugh. Too bad she was so serious and intense most of the time.

And so wrapped up in that La Amadora legend.

Josh ran behind the barn. Ahead, he saw Rose's flashlight bouncing along the trail. He caught up with her as the path plunged into a desert area thick with scrub, weeds, and saguaro cactus.

"Nothing personal," he told her, "but after today, I've seen enough cactus to last a lifetime!"

"But you haven't met my friend." She moved the beam of her flashlight to the top of a cactus. The light gleamed against three bright pink blossoms—and two beady eyes.

Josh squinted. "A bird?"

"An elf owl. He loves this saguaro."

"Cool."

Suddenly Rose laughed. "What's the matter, Josh? Too much excitement for you?" When he didn't answer, she added, "Believe me, I know how that feels. In the offseason, this ranch is a hundred acres of boredom."

She moved her flashlight to the trail. Josh fell into step beside her.

"When they started the dig a few months back, I was thrilled. At least something was happening. There were people around all the time."

Josh thought about the excavation site. "I'd love to have a dig near my house."

He wondered if Roberto would ever let him back on the site. "What's the story with Roberto? Does he ever lighten up?"

"Roberto? So he *is* angry at you. I thought I noticed something going on."

"Yeah, he's angry," Josh muttered. "I broke a piece of pottery. It was an accident. But I found it near the site, and Roberto thinks it might be Hohokam."

"*What*?" Rose spun around and grabbed his arms.

"He's not sure. Anyway, he's having it checked out."

"You went to the site?" Rose's eyes went wide.

"Last night. A few of us couldn't sleep."

"Unbelievable!" Rose stared into his eyes. "What were you thinking? Don't you know how dangerous that is?"

Josh shrugged. "We were curious."

"Curious? No," she said flatly. "You are crazy. Loco. Out of your mind! Do you know what La Amadora could do to you?"

"Rose . . ." What could he say? "It's one thing to get into history and legends. But to believe it . . . How can you fall for that stuff?"

"I don't have a choice." She lowered her eyes to the ground. "You know, I'm pretty smart. I don't believe every old legend I hear."

She sighed. "And I didn't always believe in La Amadora."

"So why do you?" Josh interrupted.

She paused, as if deciding whether she could confide in him or not. "Because La Amadora came after me," she whispered finally. "I'm lucky I got away."

Josh frowned. "Come on, Rose."

"It's true," she insisted. "I was at Signal Hill, part of a National Park, not far from here. Many of the rocks there are etched with Hohokam petroglyphs."

"Really?" That was something Josh wanted to see.

Rose nodded. "The symbols are chipped through a brown glaze. Pictures of personal accounts. Visions. No one is completely sure what they all mean."

"How cool is that?" Josh said. "If I lived here, I'd be checking out stuff like that. Not ghost legends."

"Would you listen to me?" Rose demanded. "La Amadora is not a ghost. She's a Hohokam spirit."

"Right. Was she wearing her red cape?" Josh asked.

Rose frowned at him. "If you're not going to believe me, then forget it."

"No. Go ahead," Josh insisted. "I'm sorry. Tell me what happened."

"It was getting dark, and I moved off the trail to search for other petroglyphs. I heard this noise—like someone wailing."

Josh bit his lower lip. That was the sound he'd heard, the night he arrived at the ranch.

"I should have gone back to the trail but—I don't know," Rose continued. "I thought it was the wind. Then a coyote came out of nowhere. Blocking the trail. Growling. He attacked me. He bit my arm." She clasped one hand around her arm, just below the elbow.

"Rose, it didn't have to be a spirit. Coyotes have been known to attack people," Josh said.

She shook her head. "But this was different. When I screamed, the coyote disappeared. In a flash. And all that was left, was this!" She held up her arm.

Josh saw the jagged line of a scar there.

"It didn't bleed. It was totally healed. But the scar was unmistakable. For some reason, she let me go. But she could have killed me. I came so close to—to—" Rose started to tremble.

"It's okay," Josh said, pulling her into his arms. "You're safe now." He held her close, wanting to protect her.

He ran a hand over the dark hair that cascaded over his denim jacket. So soft. So smooth.

When Rose lifted her pretty face, Josh couldn't resist.

He leaned down and kissed her.

Josh lost himself in the soft warmth of her lips. The smooth silk of her hair. The curve of her shoulders underneath her jacket.

Returning his kiss, she slid her hands around his back and hugged him.

"Oh, Josh," she whispered. "I'm so glad you're here."

"Me, too."

Her green eyes sparkled as she grinned. "You know, there was something else I wanted to show you."

"Oh, yeah?"

She pulled away and pointed her flashlight to a shaded area between two cacti. "And it's right over . . . here!" she called, darting off.

"Rose . . . where are you going?"

"You have to catch me first!" she called.

Josh laughed as he plunged into the darkness. "It's a little late for a race!"

"Come on!" she shouted.

He chased the sound of her voice to a clump of bushes. They bristled against his arms as he pushed past and waited.

Where was she?

There—a slender shadow in the distance.

He ran up to it—and skidded to a halt.

Not Rose. A slender cactus.

"Rose?" he called. "Where are you?"

Silence.

Then, footsteps.

He spun toward the noise. "Rose?"

No answer.

She was gone. And where was the trail?

Josh retraced his steps. He jogged past a familiar clump of cacti, searching for the trail.

Where was it? Where *was* it?

It should be here, right under his feet. But there were only stones and weeds and sand.

He was lost. Alone in the desert at night. Alone—except for that soft noise—breathing.

"Rose?" he called.

Silence.

The sound came from a clump of boulders. Josh went over and squatted beside them. Was Rose hiding on the other side?

"Come out, come out, wherever you are," he chanted.

A sudden movement caught his eye.

Then a growl. Vicious.

Turning, Josh stared into two shiny eyes.

The eyes of a coyote.

Chapter Twenty-three

Run, Josh, Run!

"**H**ey!" Josh let out a cry as the coyote leaped.

Its paws raked his shoulders. The animal hit with surprising force.

Josh toppled over backward. He felt his breath whoosh out.

He gasped for air as the animal's claws cut through his jacket, into his chest.

Black eyes flashing, the coyote opened its mouth in a low, ugly growl—and sank its fangs into Josh's denim jacket.

"No!" Josh kicked and pushed. He gripped the animal's head with both hands.

"Help!" he shouted.

As if someone would hear him. As if he had a chance of surviving this battle.

"Help me . . . Rose!"

Where was she?

Josh rolled to his side and shoved with all his strength. The coyote bounced into the dirt.

Yes! Josh scrambled breathlessly to his feet. He had to get away.

Where was the coyote?

He didn't see it now.

He took off. Sprinting like a racer.

One. Two. Three steps and—

"Nooooo—"

The coyote leaped at his chest. Knocked him over again. Growling in a rage. Tearing at Josh's jacket. His shirt.

Josh rolled to the side, but the coyote dug in and clung to his chest. He tried to kick it away. He rolled back and forth.

The creature stayed on him, waiting him out.

Josh was pinned down.

Trapped.

The full weight of the coyote pushed down on his chest. Claws raked him, again and again.

The coyote uttered another growl.

Its hot breath was sickening as the jaws opened.

Lowered . . . lowered . . . and . . .

"Noooooo!" Josh let out a howl of horror as sharp fangs pressed into his face.

Chapter Twenty-four

Coincidence?

BAM! BAM!
Two sharp sounds rang out above Josh.

Josh gasped as the coyote's eyes grew wide. It uttered a shrill cry—then slumped on Josh's chest and didn't move.

Josh felt something warm trickle onto his neck. Coyote blood. He pushed the coyote aside and sat up.

"Josh! What are you doing out here?"

Feeling weak and dazed, Josh squinted into the darkness—and spotted Simon. A rifle rested on his shoulder, still aimed in Josh's direction.

So it was Simon, Josh realized. A bullet fired by Simon saved my life.

"I was hiking—with Rose," Josh explained. "But we got separated."

He touched his face. No cuts. But he couldn't stop shaking—his whole body was trembling. His chest ached from the animal scratches. His denim jacket—it was shredded.

"The coyote—attacked me," Josh choked out. He swallowed. His throat felt as dry as cotton.

Simon shook his head. "Where's your flashlight? The light usually scares off coyotes. And rattlers and Gila monsters."

Touching the torn flaps of his jacket, Josh frowned. "Rose has the light. But . . . we got split up. We . . ."

"Josh!" Rose ran into the clearing. "What happened? Oh, no!"

"I tried to make friends with a coyote," Josh muttered. "It didn't work out. Your dad came to the rescue."

He stood up, shakily, feeling dizzy, drenched in sweat. "What happened to you? Where were you, Rose?"

She shrugged. "I lost you when you started running. I went back to the trail and waited, but you never showed."

"Come on," Simon said. "The jeep is parked on the trail."

"I can't believe this happened," Rose said, placing a hand tenderly on the torn sleeve of Josh's jacket. "Are you okay?"

Josh nodded. "I guess." He swallowed again. "Tough coyote. Man!"

Slinging his rifle over his shoulder, Simon scowled. "You're both to blame. The desert is

133

no place to play games. No place to take chances."

Rose stared down at the ground. "Sorry, Dad."

"You should be." Simon swung his gaze to Josh. "And you . . . you're lucky my night patrol got me here at the right time. A few minutes later and you'd have been . . ."

"I know," Josh interrupted. "Roadkill."

"The desert can be ruthless," Simon murmured. "Unforgiving."

"Just like La Amadora," Rose said wistfully.

Josh didn't argue. He wasn't sure what to believe. Silently he sank into the passenger seat of the jeep.

Rose leaned forward from the backseat. "I'm so glad you're okay," she whispered. "I can't believe I lost you back there."

"It's okay . . . now," Josh replied wearily.

"So many animal attacks," Rose murmured thoughtfully. "I hope it's all coincidence. I really hope so."

Her words rang in Josh's ears. Of course it was a coincidence. It had to be. There was no such thing as ghosts. Right?

Okay, he wasn't so sure anymore. In fact, La Amadora was beginning to make sense. How else could you explain all the animal attacks in such a short time?

Josh stared out as the jeep rumbled past towering saguaro cacti. So tall and slender. In the pale moonlight they looked like humans reaching their arms to the sky.

Simon drove up to the west patio and waited while Josh and Rose climbed out of the jeep.

"Looks like your friends are still out," Simon observed.

"I think there's a double feature at the drive-in," Rose said.

"Well, it's late. Do you need to have those scratches treated?" he asked Josh.

"I think I'm okay," Josh replied. "My jacket took most of the damage."

"Then I'd better get back to the night patrol." Simon shifted gears and held up his hand. "See you in the morning."

"Good night, Dad," Rose called after him. They watched him drive off.

"I've gotta go," Rose said. She stepped up to Josh and lifted a flap on his shredded jacket. "I'm so glad you're okay. When I think of what could have happened . . ." She squeezed her eyes shut.

"Hey, I'm okay." Josh slid his arms around her waist and pulled her close. He kissed her.

She held tight to his shoulders, returning the kiss. Then she sighed and leaned away.

"I've really gotta go," she said in a whisper. "See you in the morning."

"See you."

Josh watched as she headed down the ivy-lined path to the east wing, where the staff lived.

She likes me, he decided.

Awesome.

Now, if he could just shake this weird feeling.

This feeling that a legend that didn't make sense was starting to make perfect sense.

There was something in the eyes of that coyote—a look that was almost human. Josh shuddered.

It's too quiet now, he thought. Too empty. He wished Mickey would get back.

Opening the door to his room, Josh flipped on the light. He stepped in—

And gasped in shock.

Chapter Twenty-five

A Flash of Red

His room . . .

Mattresses and sheets were ripped off the beds. Dresser drawers were pulled out and overturned. Shoes and clothes and blankets were strewn all over the room.

Someone had totally trashed the place.

Josh disgustedly picked up a T-shirt and heaved it across the room. He shook his head. Who did this?

Why?

He gritted his teeth. Okay, this was getting weird.

Too weird.

Glancing across to the half-open closet, he froze. What if they hadn't finished? Was someone still in the room?

His heart pounding, Josh made a quick search. No one behind the overturned mattresses. And the closets . . .

Just a pile of clothes.

The curtains. . . ? He pulled back one billowing drape. He hit a bulge at the bottom and jumped back in alarm.

Nothing happened.

Bracing himself, Josh prodded it again.

Clay's duffel bag. Right where Josh had left it. But wait—the bag was open, the zipper jammed on a shirt.

Okay, the intruder was gone.

But what was he searching for? Something in the duffel bag?

The gun?

Josh grabbed up the duffel bag. Pulled out T-shirts. Balled-up socks.

And the gun spilled out.

"Huh?" Josh frowned. So . . . the intruder *wasn't* searching for the gun?

What else could someone hope to find in here? It didn't make sense.

Straightening up, Josh stared out the window. He had left it open and unlocked. People at the ranch left their doors and windows unlocked. Trisha had told them that they'd never had a problem.

Until now, Josh thought, feeling a chill.

Outside, clouds shifted. Moonlight glazed the landscape.

Light streamed out from the east patio. The screen door opened—and Josh saw Roberto emerge.

Josh watched him amble down the path,

then climb into his car. Headlights flicked on, and the car disappeared down the tree-lined lane.

Roberto? Was he here all by himself? Josh wondered.

Turning back to the mess, Josh chewed his bottom lip thoughtfully. Yes. The ranch had been empty. Trisha was still at the hospital. Rose had been with Josh. Everyone else was at the movies.

So . . . Roberto could have easily slipped in to trash the room. But why would he do it?

As Josh tossed shoes back into the closet, he thought about the broken pottery. Roberto was definitely angry about that.

But was he angry enough to do a childish thing like this?

Yawning, Josh flipped one mattress back onto the frame and fixed the sheets. He suddenly felt so weary . . . so exhausted.

Wrestling with a coyote really takes it out of you, he thought as he climbed into bed without even undressing.

He felt achy and sore. My brain is fried, he decided. I can't think straight.

Nothing makes sense. Who was here? Who is out to get me?

He yawned again. Closed his heavy eyelids.

I'll figure it all out tomorrow. . . .

Something stirred, interrupting his sleep. Josh rolled over.

"Mickey?" Josh opened his eyes.

The room was all shadows and gray shapes.

And one shape was moving. Gliding toward him fast.

"You had no right. . . ." a hoarse voice whispered.

"Mickey?" A wave of alarm shot through Josh.

"No right . . ." the voice rasped.

"What?" Josh sprang up and huddled against the wall.

"Who are you? What are you doing here?" he gasped.

Josh couldn't see the face—just a flash of red.

A red hood? La Amadora?

Then something gleamed silver in the intruder's hand.

A knife.

"Whoa!" Josh gasped. "No—please!"

PART SIX

Chapter Twenty-six

Tim and Evan are Evil

J osie had to confront Tim and Evan.

The next time she and Jennifer saw them was at a picnic at the edge of the Fear Street Woods.

A beautiful spring day. The freshly sprouted leaves shimmered so green in the bright sunlight. Blue and yellow wildflowers were sprinkled through the grass.

A checkered tablecloth spread out under an old-fashioned, wooden picnic basket. Sandwiches and potato salad. Big bags of chips.

Such a pretty scene. Such a happy moment. The four of them stretched out around the tablecloth, so relaxed, so serene.

But Josie had to confront them.

She couldn't really relax until she knew the truth.

"Are you the guys with the red paint?"

Her voice sounded colder than she intended. Yes, she had to ask. But she didn't want to accuse them if they didn't know anything about it.

Tim raised one hand to shield his eyes from the bright sunlight. He squinted across the tablecloth at Josie. "Red paint?"

Josie nodded. She saw Jennifer's smile fade.

Josie didn't back down. "Are you the ones who keep scrawling the words in red paint?"

Tim and Evan exchanged glances. Evan's expression said: *Is she crazy?*

"Someone is doing it!" Josie cried, her voice growing shrill. "Someone is sending ugly messages to me. Is it you? Is it?"

"Josie—take it easy," Jennifer urged, sitting up, her face filled with concern. "Tim and Evan don't know anything about the messages."

"Of course we do," Tim said.

Evan nodded. "Yes, we do know about them." A strange, half-smile formed on his handsome face. His dark eyes went silvery in the sunlight.

"You—you wrote them?" Josie stammered, feeling a wave of cold fear wash over her.

"Of course we did," Tim replied. He jumped to his feet, his shoes on the edge of the tablecloth.

Evan stood up, too. "Of course we wrote the messages, Josie," he said. And as he spoke, his voice lowered to a growl, lowered . . . lowered . . . to a monstrous, inhuman growl.

Josie tried to jump up. But her fear froze her

in place. "No—!" she cried. "No—!"

Tim and Evan had the same evil smile now. And their eyes glowed like silver marbles.

"Yesssss!" they both hissed. "Yesssss!"

And as Josie stared up in horror, the two boys put their arms around each other's shoulders . . . floated up . . . floated off the ground . . . over the checkered tablecloth.

And melted together.

Melted into a single figure.

Melted under a flowing, red cloak. And then a yellowed skull grinned out at Josie from under a bloodred hood. The toothless jaws tilting open in a hideous, silent laugh.

The evil spirit! Josie realized. The spirit I unleashed.

No boys. No Tim. No Evan.

It's been the evil spirit all along.

The scarlet hood fell back, revealing the rutted, yellow skull. The jaws rattled up and down, as the evil figure floated above her, laughing silently . . . laughing . . . laughing.

Chapter Twenty-seven

Tell the Truth

"Josie—what's wrong? What are you doing here?" Jennifer cried.

"I have to talk to you," Josie replied, unable to keep her voice from trembling.

Josie stood in the doorway of Jennifer's bedroom. Jennifer was in a white bathrobe, her hair still wet from the shower. She picked up a towel and began rubbing it over her hair.

"I had a dream—" Josie started.

Jennifer raised her face from under the towel. "A dream? You ran over here at eight in the morning to tell me about a dream?"

Josie crossed the room and dropped down onto Jennifer's unmade bed. "It was horrible. I think it was more than a dream. I think. . . ." She hesitated.

Josie had never told a soul about the evil spirit.

Should she tell Jennifer? Should she finally confess to someone?

She watched her friend towel off her hair. Jennifer is the only one who can help, Josie told herself. She is a Fear. She doesn't want to admit it. But she must have the powers of the Fear family.

Jennifer pulled on a sleeveless T-shirt and a pair of baggy khaki shorts. "Calm down, Josie. Take a breath. Have you had breakfast?"

"No," Josie replied. "I woke up from the dream. I ran right over."

"Come on downstairs." Jennifer led the way to the kitchen. "I'll make some coffee. We can talk."

Josie followed her, feeling shaky, tense. "Where are your parents, Jen?"

"I don't know and I don't care," Jennifer snapped. "They've been such a total pain." She poured water into the coffeemaker. She carried milk and a box of cornflakes to the breakfast table. Then she motioned for Josie to sit down. "Okay. Tell me about this horrible dream."

Josie took a deep breath and started from the beginning. She told Jennifer about the picnic, the two boys, how she confronted them, how they changed into the evil spirit.

"The *what*?" Jennifer demanded, nearly dropping the orange juice carton.

Josie hesitated. I have to tell her, she decided. I have no choice now.

"I know you're not going to believe this," she began, "but you have to try. Remember that

147

afternoon Deirdre and I were over here? And we went into that little library of yours and started fooling around with spells?"

Jennifer nodded, her eyes narrowed intently on Josie. "Go on."

"I—I never told you," Josie continued. "But when you and Deirdre left, I performed a doom spell."

Jennifer started to laugh.

But Josie cut her off quickly. "No. Really. Listen to me, Jen. It—it's too horrible. I called up some kind of evil spirit. I doomed our whole class. I—"

Jennifer rolled her eyes. "Josie—give me a break!"

"*Listen to me!*" Josie shrieked, jumping to her feet. "*You've got to believe me, Jen! You're my only hope!*"

Startled by Josie's outburst, Jennifer's mouth dropped open. "Okay, okay. You called up an evil spirit. But—"

"It's out there," Josie said, her entire body shuddering. "I've been so frightened. . . . ever since that day. Then last night, that dream . . . I don't think it was a dream. I think it was a *message* from the evil spirit."

Jennifer squinted at her. "A message?"

"The spirit is playing with me. Giving me a warning. Telling me that it is near. Telling me that Tim and Evan are evil!"

"That's impossible!" Jennifer declared. "They're two normal guys. You're talking crazy, Josie. You—"

"Try to believe me," Josie pleaded, grabbing her friend's hand. "Jennifer, I did it here, in your house. You've got to believe me. You're a *Fear*. You know that evil like this really exists."

Jennifer pulled her hand away. Her eyes locked on Josie's. She sighed. "I have something to tell you, too," Jennifer said softly. "Something I haven't told anyone."

Josie swallowed. "Huh?"

"I'm not a Fear!" Jennifer blurted out.

Josie didn't react. The words didn't make any sense.

"I'm not really a Fear," Jennifer repeated. "My family—we're no relation to the Fears at all. My grandfather took the name Fear when he moved here."

"But—why?" Josie demanded, her head spinning.

"The Fear family was the oldest and most respected family in Shadyside then," Jennifer explained. "So my grandfather just adopted their name. Do you believe it?"

"No. I don't," Josie murmured. "Then that means you have no powers. . . ."

"That's what I have been fighting with my parents about," Jennifer said, frowning angrily. "Why did they keep the name? Why didn't they change it back? Everyone in Shadyside *hates* the Fear family! Why did I have to grow up thinking I was weird, thinking my whole life that maybe I was evil? I'm so furious!"

"Wow," Josie whispered, shaking her head. "This is all too much. Too much . . . "

"There's more," Jennifer revealed. "Trisha Conrad *is* a Fear!"

Josie nearly choked.

"Trisha Conrad is actually a descendant of the Fears," Jennifer repeated. "It's true. That's probably why she's always having those psychic flashes, always having those wild visions of the future. Right?"

Josie was too shocked to answer.

"You should talk to Trisha about your evil spirit," Jennifer suggested. "Not me."

"You know she's in Arizona." Josie sighed. She gripped Jennifer's hand again. "But do you believe me? *Do* you?"

Jennifer hesitated. "I guess," she replied finally. "But what are we going to do about it? What *can* we do?"

"First, I'm going to call Tim," Josie said, jumping up and starting across the kitchen to the phone. "I'm going to confront him. I'm going to ask him the truth."

Just as I did in my dream, Josie thought.

"You can't call him now!" Jennifer declared. "It's eight o'clock in the morning. You'll wake him up. He'll—"

"I don't care!" Josie cried. "I—I'm so frightened, Jen. I have to know the truth!"

She fumbled in her bag for the piece of paper she had written Tim's phone number on. Then she punched in the number with a trembling hand.

After the fourth ring, a boy's voice answered with a sleepy "Hello?"

"Tim, it's me, Josie," she said breathlessly. "Sorry to wake you. I have to know—did you and Evan write those messages in red paint?"

She waited for a reply, her heart pounding.

"Yes," he replied finally, clearing his throat. "Yes, we did."

Chapter Twenty-eight

"Those Creeps!"

Josie uttered a sharp cry. "You mean—?"

She heard snickering laughter at the other end.

"I'm sorry. This isn't Tim," the voice said in her ear. "This is his roommate Colin. I'm not really awake. I don't know *what* I'm saying."

Josie opened her mouth to speak. But her voice caught in her throat.

"Do you want me to wake Tim up?" Colin asked.

"Yes. Please," Josie replied shakily. She took a deep breath. Tried to force her heart to stop racing.

A few seconds later Tim came on the line, sounding just as sleepy as his roommate. Josie apologized again for calling so early. Then she repeated her question about the ugly messages in red paint.

Tim was silent for a long moment. "What messages?" he replied finally. "Josie, has someone been sending you messages?"

"You don't know anything about it?" Josie demanded, starting to feel relieved.

"No. No, I don't," Tim said. "I really don't—" He stopped. "Uh, Josie? Can you hold on a second? My call waiting is beeping."

Josie heard a loud click. The line went dead.

She turned to Jennifer at the kitchen table. "Tim says he doesn't know anything about the messages."

"Of course not," Jennifer replied. "I told you—he and Evan are okay guys."

Another click, and Tim came back on the line. "Can I call you back later, Josie? I have another call I have to take."

"Yeah. Sure. Bye."

Josie started to hang up the phone. But then she heard a familiar voice come on the line. "Who were you talking to, Tim?"

Then she heard Tim reply: "Josie. She's starting to suspect something."

Tim was talking to Evan. And Josie could hear them. Some kind of call-waiting mixup. She was still on the line!

She held her breath and listened.

"What does she suspect?" Evan asked. "That we're trying to scare them?"

"Yeah," Tim replied. "She asked me about the WANNA PLAY messages. I acted real innocent."

Josie heard Evan laugh. "Do we have a plan for tonight?" he asked Tim.

"I'm going to call Josie later," Tim answered. "Invite her and her friend to climb to the top of Copple Tower with us. You know. Way up high. A historic old building. A romantic view of the whole campus . . . "

"And then what?" Evan asked. "We lock them up in there?"

Tim laughed. "Yeah. We make some excuse to leave. We lock them in the tower. Then a little while later we rescue them. And they're so grateful, they're all over us!"

They both laughed.

"The more we scare them, the hotter they are for our bods!" Tim declared.

More nasty laughter.

Seething with anger, Josie gripped the phone so tightly, her hand ached.

"What's going on?" Jennifer asked.

Josie carefully clicked off the phone and set it on the counter. Her hands were balled into tight fists as she made her way back to Jennifer.

"Creeps!" Josie screamed at the top of her lungs. "They're both *creeps*!" She tugged at her hair with both hands. "I don't *believe* it!"

"Sit down! Sit down!" Jennifer pulled her down into a chair. "What happened? Why are you freaking out?"

"It was all a trick!" Josie cried. "All a dumb, stupid trick to fool us. Some new way these creeps were trying to get girls! And we—we fell for it!"

"Josie—I don't understand! Tell me what you

heard!" Jennifer pleaded.

"Tim really did push me off the cliff," Josie said, shaking her head, her voice trembling with anger. "And then he caught me. So I'd be so grateful to him!"

Josie pounded her fist on the table. "It had nothing to do with the evil spirit! Nothing at all. Tim and Evan—they've been trying to scare us. Scare us—then rescue us. It's all a stupid trick to get us to think they're great guys!"

"Oh, wow," Jennifer moaned, suddenly pale. "Oh, wow." She raised her eyes to Josie. "What are we going to do?"

"Don't worry," Josie replied. "I've got a plan."

PART SEVEN

Chapter Twenty-nine

The Horror is Clear

o—please!" Josh shrieked.

The figure in red dived across the dark room toward him.

Josh stared at the knife blade, catching the glint of the moonlight through the window.

With a desperate cry, Josh leaped at the intruder.

Missed.

He fell heavily to the hardwood floor. His hand grappled with something solid under material.

He pulled hard. The quilt from Mickey's bed fell on top of him. Great. He had hit the bed instead of the intruder.

Josh threw the quilt aside and braced himself for the sickening flash of the knife.

He sprang up quickly, tensing every muscle, preparing to fight.

But where was his attacker?

"Hey—" Josh gasped.

Panting like an animal, he frantically searched the dark room.

Empty. No one there.

Was it a dream?

No. No way. He pictured the gleaming knife blade again. And the red cloak.

Red cloak . . . Was it La Amadora?

Josh shook his head, feeling dazed, dizzy.

He lurched to the window. Outside the stillness was broken by a muffled sound—the flurry of footsteps.

He caught a flash of someone ducking behind a trellis covered with thick flowering vines.

Hmmm. La Amadora?

Josh shook his head. That didn't sound like a ghost or a spirit. Those footsteps were solid and real.

Did that mean someone here at the ranch was trying to *kill* him?

What had the intruder said?

"You had no right . . ."

What does that mean? Josh wondered. What did I do?

When he woke up the next morning, Mickey's bed was empty.

Josh grabbed some toast in the kitchen and headed over to the corral. He was glad to see Trisha straddling the fence. Her brown eyes were bright again, her cheeks tinged with pink.

Gary sat beside her, chewing on a stalk of hay.

"You look a lot better than yesterday," Josh told her.

"I feel fine. Where's Mickey?" Trisha asked. "Don't tell me he's weaseling out of horseback-riding lessons."

Josh shrugged. "I haven't seen him. He was gone when I woke up."

"He's in the game room, playing Space Crunchers," Deirdre said, appearing from behind the barn. "He won't come out until he breaks his own record. Something about decimating twenty-five Thorzacks."

Josh stood back as two ranch hands strode out of the barn with saddled horses.

"I can't believe he's going to miss horseback riding," Trisha said. "Is he afraid of making a fool of himself?"

"Not Mickey," Gary joked. "He *always* looks like a fool."

Simon came up to Josh and handed him the reins of an Appaloosa.

The horse snorted.

Josh stared into the horse's round, watery eyes, then glanced back at Simon.

"*I'm* riding *that*? Alone? What about the lesson part?"

Simon grinned. "I'm going along. Someone's got to look out for the horses."

As his friends were paired off with horses, Josh saw Rose gallop up the hill atop a chestnut mare. Her dark hair flew behind her as she moved so easily with the horse.

She's an expert rider, Josh realized. Now he had even more to be self-conscious about.

Simon went over a few riding basics. Mounting and dismounting. How to signal the horse to stop or turn.

Josh tried to pay attention while Simon and Rose demonstrated. He did his best to keep up with the group as they set off on the trail toward Blue Rock Canyon.

But his thoughts were scattered.

Something strange was going on. Something dangerous.

And he was in the middle of it.

It wasn't just the stranger in his room last night. There was the coyote attack. The rattlesnake. And what about the first night, when he fell into that ditch at the dig?

Actually, he didn't fall. Someone pushed him.

Who? Who was after him . . . and why?

Josh's horse plodded past a cluster of cacti—fat barrel cacti, saguaros, and prickly pears. The trail rose steadily up a slope of eroded rock, gravel, and clay.

"The trail narrows from here on," Rose called back to the group. "You need to go single file."

The line of horses stretched out.

Josh sucked in his breath as the trail rose higher. They must have been climbing for at least a mile.

Just in front of Josh, Rose's horse rounded a bend.

Josh's horse moved up the ridge—then came to a sudden halt.

"Whoa!" Josh held on to the saddle horn as the horse lifted its front legs.

Behind him the other horses reacted. They reared and whinnied.

"What's happening?" Deirdre shouted.

"Whoa! Steady, now!" Simon commanded. He rode up alongside them, reaching over to calm the other horses.

"They're going wild!" Gary yelled. "What's their problem?"

"The horses know the trail," Simon explained. "They know we're coming to a sheer drop in the canyon."

Rose's horse trotted back to the group. "Just take it slow," she told them. "A few more steps."

The horses followed her instructions. Cautiously they stepped forward. One, two, three steps . . .

And Josh gasped as the earth opened up beneath them.

They stood at the lip of a high ridge. Below them—a beautiful but sheer drop to the red rocks and desert.

"Okay," Josh said, swallowing hard as he stared down. "If I knew the trail, I would be nervous, too."

They all gasped as their horses lined up, treading carefully on the ground.

"It's awesome," Gary agreed.

"Totally." Deirdre's eyes were wide with fear

as she glanced down. "Simon, are you sure this ridge can hold all of us?"

Simon nodded. "Although you see layers of clay, there's solid rock under us."

Trisha shook her head. Her brown eyes turned serious. Suddenly frightened.

"Are you okay?" Josh asked her.

"Now I remember!" Trisha clasped a hand to one cheek. "My vision!"

Josh measured the distance between Trisha and the cliff. If she fainted now . . . If she fell off her horse . . . was she far enough from the edge of the ridge?

"Another vision?" Deirdre's voice was full of fear.

"No, no, no!" Trisha touched her brow, then turned to the others. "The vision I had just yesterday! We were flying—all of us! And we were over this canyon. Here."

"A lot of the canyons look alike," Josh said softly.

Trisha's eyes darkened. "No. This is the place," she insisted. She pressed a hand to her cheek as she let her gaze drop down. . . .

Down the steep cliff. "And that's where we end up!" she cried. "I saw it so clearly. That's where we end up."

Chapter Thirty

Mickey is Dead

Trisha shivered in terror as she hunched forward in the saddle.

A sinking feeling swept over Josh as he watched her. Trisha was so sure her visions were real.

Josh wasn't convinced. But he was sure that something was wrong at the Hohokam Ranch.

"This is too scary!" Deirdre wailed. "I want to go home!"

"Come on, guys," Gary yanked the reins on her horse, trying to lead him away from the bluff. "Let's get out of here!"

"Take it easy," Rose said, moving her mare alongside Gary's horse. "You'll frighten the horses."

"But we have to get out of here!" Deirdre shrieked.

One of the horses scrambled on the ridge,

kicking up dust and stones.

Suddenly all the horses were shuffling, bodies shivering, nervous. Did they sense that something was wrong?

Josh tried to fight off his panic. He dug his knees into the horse's sides, and held on to the saddle horn tightly.

A stampede would definitely send them all tumbling over the edge.

"Okay, okay." Simon tried to soothe them all. "We'll go back. But you need to turn your horses—*one at a time.*"

Silently they followed Simon's instructions. "This is a routine ride for the horses," Simon reassured them. "You'll be fine."

Josh clung to the reins as they descended the long, narrow slope. The horses might be okay. But he wasn't so sure about his friends.

Or himself.

A short while later everyone cheered when the familiar green lawns of the ranch complex came into view.

"We're going to have lunch by the pool," Trisha announced. "Sandwiches and lemonade."

"And how about some tennis?" Deirdre suggested. "You should probably hang close to the ranch, Trisha."

"Yeah," Gary agreed. "Give yourself a chance to recover from that snake bite."

I wish it were that simple, Josh thought as he handed his horse over to a ranch hand. They were up against something worse than a rattlesnake.

But who?

Determined to find some answers, Josh headed to the game room. He wanted to run some stuff by Mickey. Josh kept hitting dead ends, but Mickey would have his own take on the situation.

The game room was empty. Silent.

Josh swept past the pools and the TV room. No sign of Mickey. He probably went back to the room, Josh decided.

Pushing open the door, Josh found the room dark. What was that lump in Mickey's bed? Was it Mickey?

Did Mickey go to sleep in the middle of the day?

"Mickey! Wake up, man. You can nap by the pool."

Mickey didn't stir. He was out, covered by the quilt, his baseball cap pulled down over his face.

"Mickey—what's your problem?" Josh was about to give Mickey a shove when he saw it—

The knife.

Buried to the hilt in Mickey's chest.

Chapter Thirty-one

Something's Out There

"**M**ickey!" Josh shrieked.

He gaped in horror at the knife blade, standing so straight.

No blood . . . no blood . . .

"Mickey—?"

Josh's stomach heaved. His knees started to collapse.

"Mickey—?"

Josh stumbled forward. Grabbed up the baseball cap.

And uttered a shocked cry.

No head. No head under the cap.

With trembling hands he jerked the quilt away—to find two fat pillows.

No Mickey.

Someone had propped the pillows under the quilt. Stuck the knife in . . .

As a joke?

Or to frighten Josh?

As a warning?

Was this one of Mickey's stupid jokes? The reason he'd stayed behind while everyone else went riding?

The door creaked open. Mickey strode in with a wide grin.

"You're looking at the Space Cruncher High Commander," he declared proudly. He pulled open a dresser drawer and sorted through it. "I rule!"

"You are about to be a dead man," Josh said through gritted teeth.

Mickey swung around, confused. "Excuse me?"

Josh folded his arms. "I found the corpse. And I'm not laughing."

"What is your problem?" Mickey squinted across the room at Josh, then lowered his eyes to the bed.

"A lot of weird stuff's been happening around here, Mickey. What I don't need is one of your lame practical jokes."

"What joke?" Mickey focussed on the knife. "Hey—what's that doing there?"

"Not funny, Mickey."

"It wasn't me!" Mickey held up his hands. "I swear! I didn't do it."

Josh glanced from Mickey to the bed. For the first time he noticed a piece of white paper. A note?

He picked it up and read aloud: *"Give it back now—or this will be you."*

"What is *that* about?" Mickey demanded. "Give back *what*?"

"The duffel bag?" Josh suggested. "The gun?"

Mickey nodded. "Could be. Maybe the cowboy came after it. What's his name—Clay?" He grabbed his swimsuit and disappeared into the bathroom.

Josh gazed at the duffel bag under the window. "But the bag is here—in plain sight. He could have just taken it. Besides, I tried to give it back."

"Weird," Mickey called. "Totally weird."

"There's been some other stuff going on," Josh said. "Like, last night? When you were gone? I got back here and—"

"Hold that thought," Mickey interrupted him. "'Cause I promised Deirdre I'd show her how to do the backstroke."

Josh blinked. "Like you're an Olympic swimmer?"

"Who's talking about swimming?" Mickey hurried out the door.

That night they built another campfire near the barbecue pit. Josh had been so busy swimming and playing tennis that the day had passed quickly.

He never had a chance to talk to Mickey again. Besides, Mickey was totally wrapped up in Deirdre. Dana, her twin sister, would freak out if she could see them now, Josh thought.

Staring into the dying embers, Josh shuddered.

He was alone in this mess.

Alone. And totally in the dark.

"Bad mood?" asked a sweet voice.

Rose stood beside him.

"I'm okay."

"Walk me back to the east wing?" she asked.

"Sure." He fell into step beside her.

"What's wrong, Josh?" she asked. "You don't look like a guy on spring break."

"Maybe you can help me. You know this place. I . . . I'm in some kind of trouble," Josh revealed.

She took his arm. "I'll try to help."

He told her about the mess in his room. And the intruder with the knife. And the knife in Mickey's bed with the note.

She shook her head. "How awful. Maybe we should phone the county sheriff. It sounds serious, Josh."

They stopped in front of the east patio. Josh leaned against an adobe wall. "I don't know. I don't know what this person thinks I have."

"It has to be the gun," she said softly. "What else could it be?" She sighed. "You must be frightened. You're having a horrible time here, aren't you?"

He raised his eyes to hers. "Well, not totally. At least I met you."

She smiled, moving closer.

Josh slid his hands down her arms. Then he pulled her close and kissed her.

"Definitely not a total loss," he said quietly.

"I'm glad." She hugged him tightly. "But I'm

worried about you. I think we should call for help. I don't think you should keep this to yourself."

He kissed her again. He knew she was right. But he was afraid to get the police involved. If he handed Clay's gun over to the police, Clay would come after him for sure.

Rose whispered good night and hurried inside.

As Josh pushed away from the building, he felt the hairs rise on his arms. That weird feeling . . .

That sense that someone was watching.

He spun around.

The lawns stood empty. The flowering vines were still. Not a sound. Nothing moved.

Still . . . that feeling stuck with him as he walked back to the west wing. It was a relief to find his room quiet and empty.

No dead roommates.

No intruders.

Mickey was off with Deirdre again. Josh changed into sweats and climbed into bed.

Mickey and Deirdre Palmer . . .

What was *that* about? Josh thought as he dozed off.

Josh could imagine the look on Dana's face when she found out about her sister and her boyfriend. He was thinking about Dana, thinking about his sister, Josie, thinking about home . . . when—

BAM! BAM! BAM!

The pounding noise shook the room.

Josh bolted out of bed.

BAM! BAM!

His heart raced as he stared at the rattling door. No! Not again.

"Who is it?" he called angrily. "Who?"

Chapter **Thirty-two**

The Cowboy Returns

Terrified, Josh leaped out of bed.

"Josh! Open up, please!" a voice called.

Rose?

Throwing open the door, Josh found her hunched in the darkness. Crying.

"Oh, Josh!" she sobbed and fell into his arms.

"Rose! What is it?"

"I was—he was there—I didn't know—" she choked out.

She can't even get the words out, Josh thought. He closed the door and helped her into a chair.

"You're okay now," Josh told her. "You've got to calm down and tell me what happened."

"My room!" She took a deep breath. "When I got back to my room, he was there. Ripping it apart."

"Who?" Josh demanded. "Was it Roberto?"

She shuddered. "I don't know. He was wearing a mask. And a red sweatshirt. A sweatshirt with a hood."

Josh gasped. Was it the same person who'd been in his room? That flash of red that made him think of La Amadora?

"Did he take anything?" Josh asked her.

"I don't think so," she answered. "But he was angry. Very angry. He pushed me to the floor."

"Rose . . ." Josh touched her arm gently. "Did he hurt you?"

She shook her head. "But he said he's been watching me. He saw me with you! And he told me to give it back. He said I'd better make you give it back."

Her green eyes glistened as she fixed her gaze on Josh. "What did he mean? What is he after, Josh?"

"I don't know!" Josh insisted, turning away.

"Can't you make him go away, Josh?" Rose pleaded. "Please, give him what he wants?"

"I swear, I don't know what he's talking about. Not a clue."

Rose went to the window. "I'd better go. My father will stop by my room to say good night, and when he sees the mess . . ." She shook her head. "He's going to freak."

"I'll walk you back." Josh grabbed his sweatjacket and opened the door.

The desert air was chilling. Brisk. A cold reminder of reality.

Did Cowboy Clay want his gun? Not likely. If

it was that important, he could have just taken it from Josh's room.

Roberto. . . ?

Maybe. He was still seething over the broken pottery. Did he think Josh took something else from the site?

Who else could it be?

He walked Rose all the way to her door. She peeked inside, then turned to him. "It's all right. He didn't come back."

"Are you sure you're okay?" he asked her.

Her green eyes flashed as she reached up and hugged him. "*You're* the one I'm worried about, Josh. This guy means business."

"I knew it!" Gary raised a fist and pounded the railing. After breakfast Josh had cornered Mickey and Gary by the pool.

He wanted to confront Roberto.

And he needed some help from his friends. After all, the guy had tried to kill him.

"I knew that guy was a creep," Gary declared. "And he's not going to get away with this. Breaking into your room. Breaking into a *girl's* room!"

"Rose must have freaked," Mickey said, shaking his head.

"She was scared. And, hey, so was I," Josh admitted. "I mean, this guy trashed our room and came at me with a knife. He's not fooling around."

"Wait till Trisha finds out," Gary said. "The guy is a psycho. He's totally disturbed."

Josh knew Gary would go along with any plan to attack Roberto. He'd do anything to get Roberto away from Trisha.

"So . . .what's the plan?" Mickey asked.

"He's probably out at the excavation site," Josh said.

"Hiiyaaa!" Gary threw a karate punch in the air. "We find him. He's toast!"

The sun beat down on their shoulders as they hiked the trail. Josh was glad that he had snagged three bottles of water from the kitchen staff. They would need every drop.

Gary kicked some loose stones from the trail. "We need some dirt bikes or something."

"Yeah," Josh agreed. The heat drained everyone. But as the dig came into view, he felt a shot of energy.

Time to confront Roberto. Time to straighten things out.

He went over to a short, skinny guy in a khaki desert cap. From the way the man was shouting instructions, he seemed to be in charge.

"We're looking for Roberto Morales," Josh told him.

"Yeah, yeah, Roberto." The guy nodded. "He left about an hour ago. We needed some supplies from Tucson."

Josh frowned. "Is he coming back?"

"Roberto? I think so. I'm not sure. Simon should know. Hey—" The man tucked a clipboard under his arm and hurried down the rise. "No, no, no! You can't move those pieces until they've been photographed."

Wiping the sweat from his forehead, Josh turned to his friends. "Let's ask around back at the ranch."

Mickey adjusted his baseball cap. "Yeah, okay. The long walk back."

At the ranch they checked the pool area and the kitchen. No sign of Roberto. Inside the stables, Simon was saddling up horses.

"Where have you guys been?" he asked. "The girls have been looking for you. Trisha was ready to send out a search party."

"We've got something to take care of," Gary said.

"Have you seen Roberto?" Josh asked the foreman.

"I let him take one of our jeeps into town," Simon answered. "He'll be back after lunch."

Josh spotted Trisha and Deirdre by the door. They stepped into the shade of the barn, sipping from sodas in cans.

"We were just about to go without you," Trisha said.

"Go?" Josh glanced around. "Where?"

"For a picnic," Trisha replied. "Lunch is all packed. And Rose knows a good spot with shade and a great view."

Rose appeared behind her, lugging two satchels of food. She handed them to Simon, who packed them onto her horse.

"Food . . . food . . . food . . ." Mickey chanted, staggering stiff-legged toward Rose like a zombie.

The girls laughed.

"Shut up and get on a horse," Deirdre ordered.

Josh went over to Rose. "Are you okay?" he asked.

She spared him a quick smile. "Fine. You?"

"It's under control." He gave her a thumbs-up and hoisted himself into the leather saddle of his horse.

"Okay, we've got a trot going here," Mickey called out as his horse ambled out of the barn into the sunlight. "But how do you stop these things?" He pretended to peek under the horse's mane. "Hey! Where are the hand brakes!"

They laughed as Rose led them onto the trail. The trail that led to the canyon.

Glancing ahead, Josh was glad to see Trisha giggling. Maybe, if they kept her distracted, they wouldn't have to hear about another vision.

But the tone of the trip was different today. Mickey kept clowning around, pretending to be a total idiot when it came to horseback riding.

When the trail narrowed and rose to the steep top of the canyon, no one seemed to care.

Been there, done that, Josh thought.

"The picnic area is just beyond the ridge," Rose announced to everyone. "The view is spectacular. But there's room to spread out. And a place for the horses."

Catching the view, Mickey gasped. "Hey! We

found the end of the earth! Wow! It's awesome!"

Josh glanced down the line of horses stretched out along the ridge. For the moment things seemed back to normal again. Just a bunch of high school friends, having fun on spring break.

The steady beating sound made him turn. A horse and rider appeared down the trail— galloping way too fast.

"Who's that?" Josh asked.

Heads turned toward the approaching horse.

"It's that guy—" Mickey said. "From the plane."

Gary sneered. "That cowboy who ran us off the road!"

"Clay Hartley?" Josh gasped. "What's he doing here?"

"He didn't come for a picnic!" Gary exclaimed.

Josh turned to Rose. "Get us out of here!" he shouted.

Her face showed the strain of fear as she shook her head. "He's right on us. We can't outrun him."

Her words were nearly lost in the pounding hoofbeats of Clay's horse over the hard trail.

Through the dust Josh saw the man's face. . . .

Cruel. Cold. Angry.

Sitting straight in the saddle, he used one hand for the reins.

The other hand cradled a smooth hunk of molded steel.

A black, long-barreled rifle.

Chapter Thirty-three

Deirdre is Dead

Josh shuddered as his eyes shifted from one horror to the other.

The gun.

The sheer drop.

Take a bullet from a lunatic? Or smash onto the red rocks below?

Not a great choice.

"This is part of my parents' ranch!" Trisha shouted at Clay Hartley. "You're trespassing."

"Trespassing?" He grinned at Trisha. "Why don't you call a cop?" He swept the rifle down the line. "Everybody, off your horses," he ordered. "And let's climb down nice and slow."

"No—wait!" Rose protested. "The horses will run away."

"Tough luck," Clay muttered.

"But we'll be stranded up here!" Rose added.

Clay hitched back his Stetson hat and

scowled at her. "Do I look like someone who cares?" He waved the weapon at the group. "I said get down. Now!"

They all scrambled off their horses.

"Whoa!" Gary yelled, losing his grip. His boot stuck in one stirrup, and he flopped onto the ground face first.

Josh and Trisha rushed over to help him up.

The horses shuffled off toward the trail, restless and frightened.

"Don't do anything crazy!" Rose shouted, stepping toward Clay. "Nobody has to get hurt, right?"

No answer.

Clay glared at the group. His eyes gleamed with anger.

Rose is so brave, Josh thought. She stood up for herself. Stood up for everyone.

"Okay, kids," Clay said in a mocking voice. "We're going to play a little game called 'Line up on the Ledge.' Everyone plays. Everyone wins. Just move away from the trail and take a step back."

They had no choice. They followed his orders.

Josh fell into line between Deirdre and Rose.

"Okay, kids. Let's move back . . . back . . ." Clay ordered.

Josh felt his knees shake as the canyon came into view.

The view was spectacular. The sheer drop was terrifying.

"That's good for now," Clay said. He walked

up the line and paused in front of Josh. "The next part of our game is called 'Tell the Truth.'"

He pressed his face close to Josh's. "And you're the man. Where is it?"

Josh flinched. "I don't know what you're talking about! You're making a big mistake!"

"This is no joke! Hand it over now! Or you'll all go over the side!"

Grabbing Josh's shirt, Clay pulled him around, forcing him to stare down into the gaping canyon.

Josh uttered a frightened moan.

Just a few inches of dirt separated him from a free fall.

"Do it, Josh!" Deirdre screamed. "Do what he wants!"

"Please!" Rose begged quietly.

Josh shook his head. "I can't!" Josh protested. "I don't have it!"

"Okay!" Clay growled.

He released Josh's shirt and raised the gun again.

"Back to our game!" Clay shouted. "Everybody takes another step back. Now! Now!"

Shaking, Josh scraped his shoe back carefully. There wasn't much ground left.

He finished the step—still on solid ground.

For now.

Clay scowled, then waved the gun at the kids again.

"This is so simple! *So simple!*" Clay shouted.

"Just give me what belongs to me and—"
A scream cut him off.
A shrill, desperate cry.
Turning, Josh saw Deirdre pitch forward.
The ground beneath her crumbled away.
Her boots sank into dirt and dust.
She started to fall over the side.
Josh hit the dirt.
Reached out.
Made a wild grab for her.
Missed.

Chapter Thirty-four

Rose's Revenge

Deirdre screamed all the way down.

Josh watched helplessly as she fell, his arms dangling over the cliffside, hands still grabbing for her.

Her shrill cry rang in his ears. Echoed off the canyon walls.

It stopped with a sick *crack*.

He watched her body bounce on the rocks.

And then she didn't move.

Behind him the horrible sounds of shock and pain. Sobs and cries of disbelief.

"No!" Trisha shrieked. "Deirdre! Deirdre!"

"She's gone." Gary collapsed against Trisha, hugging her close. "She's . . . she . . ."

Mickey buried his face in his hands.

Josh curled up and glared at Clay.

The man standing in the sunlight. The man who had killed Deirdre.

Fury shot through him. Exploded inside him. Pulling him to his feet. Snapping his muscles taut. Driving him forward.

"You killed her!" Josh growled.

He didn't know what he was doing. He couldn't help himself.

"You killed her!" he shouted. He dived toward Clay, surprising him.

The rifle clattered to the ground. Clay toppled back off-balance. He landed in a cloud of dust on the trail.

His heart pounding, Josh saw his chance. He grabbed up the rifle and swung the barrel at Clay.

Clay cowered in a ball on the ground.

Josh tried to talk, but he was breathing too hard, struggling to catch his breath, his chest aching, about to explode.

"It's okay," said a soft voice. Rose's voice.

Josh felt her gentle hand on his arm.

"It's okay, Josh," she repeated. "We're safe now. I'll keep the gun on him."

Wheeling around, Josh realized that the gun was shaking in his hands. His entire body was shaking.

Deirdre is dead. . . . Deirdre is dead.

Again he heard the *crack.* Her horrifying scream—and then the *crack* when she hit the rocks.

He knew he'd hear that sound for the rest of his life.

"Over there," Rose's voice broke into his thoughts. She nodded toward the trail. "Try to round up the horses before they all get away. I'll take the gun."

The horses . . . Josh nodded.

At least Rose was in control. Thinking straight.

"Okay, here." He handed the gun to Rose and sank with relief. If he and the other guys moved fast, they might be able to catch a few of the horses.

He sprinted onto the trail.

Rose's voice cut into his thoughts.

"Not so fast."

Turning, he saw her pointing the rifle at him.

"Back in line, Josh. With everyone else," Rose ordered.

"What?" he gasped. What was she doing?

Rose held the rifle steady on him as he joined his friends.

"Okay." She turned to Clay, who had climbed to his feet and was dusting off his hat.

Rose sighed, then asked, "What are we going to do with them now, Clay?"

Chapter Thirty-five

Josh is Dead

Josh uttered a shocked cry. "Rose—?"

She ignored him, her eyes on Clay.

Josh turned to his friends. They gaped at her in disbelief.

"It was supposed to be easy," Rose told Clay. "But you pushed too far. Now there's a murder."

"An accident." Clay stepped closer to Rose, as if he didn't want Josh and the others to hear. "We didn't kill her. She fell."

"Oh, come on, Clay," Rose groaned. "That girl is dead, and we still don't have the coyote. We're still nowhere."

Clay's nostrils flared in anger.

What's he going to do now? Josh wondered.

With an animal-like growl Clay sprang on Josh. He grabbed his shirt and yanked him forward.

Josh choked as his feet dragged through the dirt.

"Where is it? Where?" Clay growled. "I left it in my duffel bag. What did you do with it?"

Squinting up into the sun, Josh could only see silhouettes. The outline of Clay swinging toward Rose, grabbing the gun away.

Suddenly Josh was staring down the shiny nose of the weapon.

"Where's the coyote?" Clay growled. He nudged the gun into Josh's chest, pushing him back into the dirt again. "Give us the coyote!"

The coyote?

Josh gaped at him. "Coyote? What are you talking about?"

"You want to play innocent?" Clay growled. "Fine. I guess I'll just have to kill all of you."

"What?" Josh scurried to his feet. "Wait!"

Clay pretended to squeeze the trigger as he picked off Josh's friends, one by one—

Mickey. Trisha. Gary.

"Whoa. Just explain something to us," Mickey demanded. "A coyote? That's what you're looking for?"

Rose's green eyes flashed. She motioned for Clay to back off.

He lowered the rifle.

Mickey pulled something out of his jeans pocket and held it up. "Is this what you're look-ing for?"

A small clay figurine, no bigger than the palm of his hand. It was buff-colored with red stripes.

A statue of a coyote.

"I found it on the west patio," Mickey

explained. "Simon told me I could keep it. So I did."

Josh stared at his friend. Mickey? Mickey had the coyote?

"I didn't know it fell out of your bag!" Mickey cried. "I was going to take it home to my girl-friend, but—"

"That's it!" Rose snatched the figurine out of his hand. "You idiot! How can you be so stupid?"

Mickey shrugged. "Hey, it's just a statue."

"It's a genuine Hohokam fetish!" Rose cried.

A fetish . . .

A consecrated object . . .

A statue inhabited by a spirit.

Or at least, that's what the Hohokam would have believed.

Josh knew enough about archaeology to figure it out. The figurine was supposed to have power, the power to aid or protect.

And that meant it was valuable.

"I just met with a dealer in New York who offered a ton of money," Clay told them.

"A million dollars," Rose boasted. "Clay and I—we're going to be millionaires. No thanks to you jerks!"

"Can we go now?" Trisha cried. "Now that you've killed our friend? Can we go?"

Rose didn't seem to hear her. She stared at the statue in the palm of her hand, as if it held her in a trance.

Josh stared at it, too.

A coyote with red stripes . . .

The vision! Josh realized. That was the image in Trisha's vision. A coyote with red stripes.

And all of us flying over this cliffside.

All of us . . .

Part of the vision had come true. Deirdre lay dead at the bottom.

And now . . . ?

Rose and Clay were arguing again.

"We've got the fetish," Rose said. "Let's grab horses and get out of here. We can be out of Arizona by nightfall."

"What about them?" Clay demanded. "You want to leave them behind? Four people who know the whole story?"

A shadow crossed Rose's face as she glanced over at Josh. "I don't know," she said quietly. "I don't know what to do now."

"I know," Clay insisted. "It's easy. They're just inches away from the answer. They'll all die in a horrible accident."

Josh felt his stomach wrench.

Rose hesitated. "Do you think so? Is that the only way?"

Clay ignored her. He turned to Josh and his friends. "Okay, who goes first?"

He pointed the gun at Josh. "Let's start with you."

Chapter Thirty-six

A Long Way Down

You'll have to shoot me! Josh thought.
I'm not going to jump.

"No!" Rose shrieked. "I can't! I can't let
you! I'm not a murderer, Clay."

"Well, too bad," Clay said. "Because I am,
you know. Remember Ben? That ranch hand
who *fell* and broke his neck at the site?"

"You killed Ben Granger," Trisha murmured.

"Did I have a choice?" Clay replied. "He
caught me at the site."

"Clay, that was never part of our plan." Rose
shuddered. "How could you?"

Clay scowled. "Did you really think his neck
was snapped by La Amadora?"

Black hair whipped over her shoulders as
Rose shook her head. "No! But I didn't agree to
killing."

"Well, it happened. And you helped with the

plan," Clay said. "I guess that makes you an accomplice."

"No!" Rose shrieked. "I didn't agree to hurt anyone! You know why I helped you steal things from the site. I just wanted out. Enough money to leave this stupid ranch."

So all the stuff about La Amadora was a setup, Josh realized. Rose didn't believe any of it. It was only a legend that Rose used to keep people away from the site at night.

And it had worked.

Almost too well. Rose probably hadn't expected so much help from the desert.

A startled rattlesnake.

A cornered coyote.

Rose and Clay had gotten help from some surprising places.

Clay remained with his legs planted firmly on the trail, the rifle pointed squarely at Josh.

"I've spent my whole life on this stupid ranch." Rose's voice cracked with emotion. "I don't want to end up here forever, like my dad." She sniffed. "But I won't kill anybody! I just won't!"

"Oh, really?" Clay's eyes glimmered. Something was brewing in his mind.

He held out his hand. "Give it to me."

"No."

Clay stepped closer to her. "I said give me the fetish, Rose. Now."

She twisted her arm around, holding the figurine behind her back. "And I said no. Who do you think—"

Clay's arm whipped out suddenly. He grabbed the statue, knocking it loose from Rose's grip.

It hit the ground. Skittered over the stone path—and slid over the side of the canyon.

"Noooo!" A furious howl escaped Clay's throat—as he dived for it.

Dived—with both hands grasping wildly.

Dived.

Over the edge of the cliff.

No!

Not again!

Without thinking, Josh dropped to the ground—and made a desperate grab for Clay.

Clay's jeans slid through his hands.

Desperately Josh tore at the fabric—

And got a grip on Clay's ankles.

He felt a hard tug as he stopped Clay from pitching forward. And then—Josh felt himself being dragged down.

"No!" he shouted, digging his knees into the dirt.

"Nooooo!"

Clay was too heavy. Too heavy.

He started to drop—and take Josh down with him.

Chapter Thirty-seven

Gone Forever

Below him, Clay sputtered as dirt slid into his face.

"No! Don't move!" Josh pleaded.

But Clay was frantic. "Get me up! Get me—"

Clay shifted one leg, and that did it.

Josh felt himself sliding forward, through the dirt—

"Whoa!" came a voice behind him.

Firm hands yanked Josh back by his belt. Josh squeezed his eyes shut and held on to Clay as someone dragged them back to safety.

A deep breath.

Then Josh turned to find Roberto standing over him.

Roberto?

Trisha and Gary huddled behind him. Rose was collapsed on the ground, sobbing.

Simon appeared. He ran over to Clay, a rifle tucked under his arm.

"What are you doing here? Are you guys crazy?" Roberto shrieked.

"Yeah," Josh said, struggling to catch his breath. "He's crazy enough to go over the cliff for an Indian statue. And I was crazy to try and save him."

"A statue?" Roberto's eyes grew wide. "From the site?"

"A striped coyote." Josh nodded toward the canyon. "He and Rose stole it. They worked together. The only thing is, it's probably in a million pieces right now."

"And Deirdre!" Trisha cried. "Deirdre is down there, too."

"I still can't believe it," Mickey said, looking lost.

Gary pointed a finger at Clay. "He killed her."

"She fell," Clay muttered.

"You *made* her fall," Gary accused.

"And he killed that ranch hand—Ben," Josh told Simon. "He told us. He was bragging about it."

Simon shook his head sadly. "I'll radio the sheriff. He'll meet us back at the ranch. And he'll send a crew to the canyon to . . . to look for her."

To pick up her body, Josh thought. That's what Simon had started to say.

But the words made everyone sick.

Deirdre was gone. Gone forever.

Simon shielded his eyes against the sun. "We

can sort the rest of this out at the ranch."

"I'll take the horses back for you," Rose offered. She held the reins of two of the horses who hadn't wandered far.

"Do you think you're getting away with this?" Simon's dark eyes were shadowed by his hat, but Josh could hear the pain in his voice.

"Do you think the police are not going to charge you because you're my daughter?" Simon asked Rose.

Dark hair fell over her face as Rose's chin tilted down. "I didn't hurt anyone," she said quietly. "Not really."

"You helped him," Gary insisted.

"It's a police matter now," Simon said. "Come on, Rose. You're riding back in the jeep with us."

"Me, too," Trisha moaned. "I don't feel too good."

"Nobody does," Gary said as he walked Trisha toward the vehicle. "Nobody."

"I'll take the horses," Roberto suggested. "Josh and Mickey can help me."

"Yeah, sure," Josh agreed. The jeep couldn't hold everyone. Besides, the farther he could stay from Clay Hartley, the better off he'd be.

The guys climbed into the saddles and pointed the horses toward the downhill trail. Roberto led the fourth horse along on a loose tether.

"What about the other loose horses?" Mickey asked.

Roberto pushed back his hat. "They'll make

it back to the stables. They know the way, and they need food and water."

For a while the only sound was the plodding of the horses. Josh sagged with relief as the trail dipped lower.

The view from that ridge was amazing. . . .

Breathtaking.

And I hope I never see it again! he swore under his breath.

As the trail rounded a bend, the dig site came into view.

Roberto reined in his horse and sighed. "I never guessed it would ever cause so much trouble," he said, staring at the site.

"How do you think they found the fetish?" Josh asked.

"Luck." Roberto frowned. "Plus the fact that they must have been raiding the site for months. They probably found other things, but nothing so valuable."

"I can't believe that coyote was worth so much," Mickey said. "I had a million dollars in my pocket! And I didn't have a clue."

"Isn't it weird that Trisha saw it in her vision?" Josh asked. "A coyote with stripes?"

Roberto shrugged. "She may have seen it in a book. Or maybe she's seen some petroglyphs. Trisha has visited Hohokam territory before."

"Or maybe she got a vision from La Amadora," Josh said sarcastically. When Roberto met his gaze, he shrugged. "Rose really played that one up."

"Still, it's a real legend," Roberto answered. "I've never seen her. But that doesn't mean she's not real."

Right, Josh thought.

Roberto turned his horse away. Josh lifted the reins and saw something moving at the site.

A flash of red?

Yes! A woman in a hooded red cloak. And she was standing next to a dog.

Josh squinted into the waves of shimmering heat.

No—not a dog. A coyote!

"Do you see that?" he cried.

"See what?" Roberto and Mickey replied in unison.

Josh squinted harder.

Gone.

She had disappeared.

Now he saw only sand. Ridges of heat.

And miles and miles of cacti. Tall and still, standing guard over the desert—and its legends.

PART EIGHT

Chapter Thirty-eight

The Last Laugh

"**W**e'll teach Tim and Evan. We'll pay them back for their dirty trick. We'll scare *them!*" Josie suggested, her eyes flashing excitedly. "Then we'll tell them to get lost."

"How do we scare them?" Jennifer asked.

"Call Dana Palmer," Josie replied. "Call some other kids from our class who are home. Tim and Evan are going to invite us to climb some old tower on the campus tonight. Instead, we tell them we'd rather go to the Fear Street Cemetery. You know. To make out. Then—"

"Okay. Fine," Jennifer interrupted. "But what do Dana and the other kids do?"

"I'm getting to that," Josie replied impatiently. "They get to the cemetery before us. They wear green makeup or something. Ragged, torn clothes. Make themselves look dead and decayed. They hide behind the old gravestones. And when we get there, they come up. They make it look like they're climbing up from the graves."

Josie grinned. "It'll be so cool!"

Jennifer grinned back at her. "It's such a dumb idea, it just might work!"

"The guys will probably run for their lives," Josie added. "And *we* won't rescue them!"

"Let's get to work," Jennifer said.

They spent the rest of the morning calling their friends, making their plans.

Jennifer was waiting at Josie's house when the van pulled up the driveway a little after eight o'clock. Josie kissed Tim on the cheek as she climbed in beside him.

After a lot of warm greetings from everyone, Tim backed the van into the street.

"We can go to that old tower later," Jennifer told Evan, getting right to the point. "Josie and I—we thought maybe you'd like to stop at the Fear Street Cemetery first," she said, lowering her voice to a kittenish whisper.

Josie saw Tim's eyes light up. She edged closer to him and placed a hand on his arm. "It's so dark and romantic there," she whispered, leaning close to him. "We can get to know each other better."

"Whoa," Tim murmured. He headed the van toward Fear Street and the old cemetery. Josie didn't have to explain anything to him. Everyone in town knew that the cemetery was a popular place for couples who wanted to be alone.

A few minutes later Tim pulled the van onto the grass at the foot of the cemetery and parked. It was a cool, crisp spring night. A light breeze rustled the fresh leaves on the ancient trees and made the heavy limbs creak.

Josie took Tim's arm. She pressed close to him as they led the way up the sloping hill toward the rows of old gravestones.

A squirrel scampered across their feet, rustling the carpet of dead leaves from the past winter. The old trees blocked the moonlight, surrounding them in darkness.

Jennifer and Evan wandered off toward the low picket fence. Josie stopped beside a tilting maple tree. She wrapped her arms around Tim's neck and raised her face to his in a tender kiss.

A few seconds later the first ghost rose up from behind a square stone monument. He had pale green skin, hair slicked back on his head, dark holes where his eyes had been.

Evan was the first to cry out. "Hey—what's that?"

Tim spun away from Josie as four other ghosts climbed into view. They all moved as if in slow motion. They stretched their arms and tilted their pale, ghastly heads, uttering low moans.

Josie stepped back and enjoyed the shocked expressions on the guys' faces. Then she turned to enjoy the moaning ghosts.

Dana Palmer is the *best*! she decided.

Dana wore a flowing white robe. Her face was so pale, it had no color at all. Her blond hair flew up around her head. And she appeared to float above the tombstone. Float up softly, the robe fluttering in the breeze. So pale . . . so ghostly pale . . .

Dana waved to them, slowly, sadly.

Fabulous, Josie thought.

She saw Tim and Evan exchange confused glances. Glimpsed the fear in their eyes. Fear mixed with suspicion.

And then all four of them screamed as Dana Palmer raised one hand—*and shoved it right through a solid granite gravestone!*

How did she *do* that? Josie wondered.

She turned to see the two guys running down the hill in terror.

"I'm outta here!" Tim cried.

"Whoa! Too weird!" Evan declared.

Josie and Jennifer started after them. But the guys didn't look back once. They dived into the van and roared off, without a thought for the two girls.

Laughing triumphantly, Josie and Jennifer slapped each other a high five. Then they hurried back up the hill to thank their friends.

"Halloween came a little early this year!" one of the ghosts cried.

"Did you see their faces? They really believed it!" another one added.

"Where's Dana?" Josie asked, searching their faces. "Dana was awesome. Where is she?"

"Maybe she went home," someone suggested.

"Yeah. She's been sick," Jennifer remembered. "The flu or something. Maybe she hurried home." She shook her head. "Dana was the best!"

As they walked to Josie's house, the two girls congratulated themselves on their victory. "They really are creeps," Josie said.

Jennifer agreed. "Good riddance."

"Why couldn't we meet *nice* guys and have a *nice* spring break?" Josie wondered.

"Hey—there's always next spring!" Jennifer exclaimed.

A few minutes later, in her room, Josie hurried to call Dana Palmer and thank her. The phone rang five times before Dana picked it up.

"Dana—you were awesome!" Josie cried. "Thanks!"

Silence on the other end. And then Dana replied, very softly, "I couldn't go, Josie. I wasn't there. Didn't you *hear* about my sister?"

Josie's heart skipped a beat. "Huh? Hear what?" she asked.

"Deirdre is *dead*, Josie. Deirdre died—in Arizona. I—I—I have to go!"

Josie heard a loud sob, and then Dana hung up.

"What's wrong?" Jennifer demanded from across the room. "Josie? What is it? What's wrong?"

Josie swallowed hard. She crossed the room, trembling, and wrapped her friend in a hug.

"Jennifer," she whispered. "I—I think Deirdre came to say good-bye to us tonight."

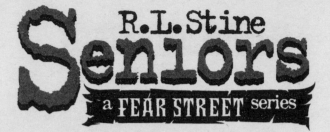

R.L. Stine
Seniors
a FEAR STREET series

available from Gold Key® Paperbacks

FEAR STREET® Sagas

available from Gold Key® Paperbacks:

Circle of Fire
Chamber of Fear
Faces of Terror
One Last Kiss
Door of Death
The Hand of Power

FEAR STREET® titles

available from Gold Key® Paperbacks:

The Stepbrother
Camp Out
Scream, Jennifer, Scream!
The Bad Girl

Do you know the address for Fear?

www.fearstreet.com

Connect to the curse of **The Fear Family** with the brand new **Fear Street Website!** This scary site brings you up close and personal with the legend of the Fears and their legacy of blood. With sneak peeks at upcoming stories, top secret information, games, gossip, and the latest R.L. Stine buzz on who will survive, this is your chance to know the deadly truth.

Get caught in the web of fear!

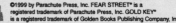

About R.L. Stine

R.L. Stine is the best-selling author in America. He has written more than one hundred scary books for young people, all of them bestsellers.

His series include *Fear Street, Fear Street Seniors,* and the *Fear Street Sagas*.

Bob grew up in Columbus, Ohio. Today he lives in New York City with his wife, Jane, his son, Matt, and his dog, Nadine.

Don't Miss FEAR STREET® Seniors
Episode Ten!

WICKED

Valedictorian.

That's all Marla Newman wants. But her chance is
quickly slipping away.

Then Marla meets two juniors who say they can give
Marla the power to get anything she wants.
Anything.

But Marla soon learns that power comes with a
price . . . paid in blood.